1763

$3.25 U.S.
$3.75 CAN.
September

HARLEQUIN ✦ PRESENTS®

CHARLOTTE LAMB

Dark Fate

Pages & Privileges ™

See inside!

You're About to Become a

Privileged Woman.

INTRODUCING
PAGES & PRIVILEGES™.

It's our way of thanking you for
buying our books at your
favorite retail store.

Pages & Privileges ™

*G*ET ALL THIS *F*REE
WITH JUST ONE PROOF OF PURCHASE:

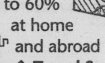

$50 VALUE

◆ **Hotel Discounts** up to 60% at home and abroad ◆ **Travel Service -** Guaranteed lowest published airfares plus 5% cash back on tickets ◆ **$25 Travel Voucher** ◆ **Sensuous Petite Parfumerie** collection ◆ **Insider Tips Letter** with sneak previews of upcoming books

You'll get a FREE personal card, too.
It's your passport to all these benefits– and to
even more great gifts & benefits to come!

There's no club to join. No purchase commitment. No obligation.

HP-PP5A

Enrollment Form

☐ *Yes!* I WANT TO BE A *P*RIVILEGED *W*OMAN.
Enclosed is one *PAGES & PRIVILEGES™* Proof of
Purchase from any Harlequin or Silhouette book currently for
sale in stores (Proofs of Purchase are found on the back pages
of books) and the store cash register receipt. Please enroll me
in *PAGES & PRIVILEGES™*. Send my Welcome Kit and FREE
Gifts – and activate my FREE benefits -- immediately.
More great gifts and benefits to come.

NAME (please print)

ADDRESS   **APT. NO**

CITY   **STATE**   **ZIP/POSTAL CODE**

| PROOF OF PURCHASE ONLY | **NO CLUB!** **NO COMMITMENT!** *Just one purchase brings you great Free Gifts and Benefits!* |

Please allow 6-8 weeks for delivery. Quantities are limited. We reserve the right to
substitute items. Enroll before October 31, 1995 and receive one full year of benefits.

Name of store where this book was purchased_____

Date of purchase_____

Type of store:

☐ Bookstore   ☐ Supermarket   ☐ Drugstore
☐ Dept. or discount store (e.g. K-Mart or Walmart)
☐ Other (specify)_____

Which Harlequin or Silhouette series do you usually read?

Complete and mail with one Proof of Purchase and store receipt to:
U.S.: *PAGES & PRIVILEGES™*, P.O. Box 1960, Danbury, CT 06813-1960
Canada: *PAGES & PRIVILEGES™*, 49-6A The Donway West, P.O. 813,
North York, ON M3C 2E8

HP-PP5B

▼ DETACH HERE AND MAIL TODAY! ▼

"Come back to me, Saskia. We can start again...."

"No! Stay away from me!"

He stopped, face taut, pale now. "Okay. But at least explain, Saskia. Don't I deserve an explanation? Why you left me? Why you won't come back?"

Her blue eyes were shadowed with pain and regret. "You know why! You want children and I couldn't, never again.... I couldn't bear it if it happened again."

He said quietly, "There's no reason why you shouldn't have a perfectly healthy baby the second time."

CHARLOTTE LAMB was born in London, England, in time for World War II, and spent most of it moving from relative to relative to escape bombing. Educated at a convent, she married a journalist, and now has five grown-up children. The family lives on the Isle of Man. Charlotte has written over one hundred books, most of them for Harlequin.

Books by Charlotte Lamb

HARLEQUIN PRESENTS
1658—FIRE IN THE BLOOD
1672—WOUNDS OF PASSION
1687—FALLING IN LOVE
1706—GUILTY LOVE
1720—VAMPIRE LOVER
1733—BODY AND SOUL
1743—DYING FOR YOU

CHARLOTTE LAMB

Dark Fate

Harlequin Books

TORONTO • NEW YORK • LONDON
AMSTERDAM • PARIS • SYDNEY • HAMBURG
STOCKHOLM • ATHENS • TOKYO • MILAN
MADRID • WARSAW • BUDAPEST • AUCKLAND

ISBN 0-373-11763-9

DARK FATE

First North American Publication 1995.

CHAPTER ONE

As THE lights went down in the theatre, Saskia suddenly knew Domenico was there.

Not only was he there, but he had seen her too, at the same moment. At the very instant that she sensed his presence she felt the surge of his rage and it was like being hit by lightning. Her whole body reacted with a jerk of terrible shock.

Sitting beside her, Jamie felt her shudder, and looked round at her, his face concerned, whispering, 'Toothache back again?'

She drew a shaky breath and lied without stopping to think.

'Just a jab; it's gone now.'

In the blueish dimness cast out into the upper reaches of the rococo theatre by the footlights she glimpsed Jamie's curly brown hair, his rugged, weatherbeaten face; and Jamie could probably see the gleam of her blue eyes, the shimmer of her skin. She bent her head and the shining bell of her dark auburn hair fell forward so that he couldn't see anything more of her. It was instinctive, to hide her expression and the feelings she was afraid might show in it; Jamie knew very little about her—she had only ever told him what she felt he really needed to know, and she didn't want him to know any more, especially about Domenico.

'Sure?' Jamie whispered, leaning closer. 'If you need them, I've got some paracetamol in my pocket. I thought they might come in useful in case your tooth started playing up again.'

That was typical of Jamie, not only because he was warmly sympathetic to anyone in pain, but because he was so intensely practical and thoughtful in the way he responded. Jamie never simply used words; he immediately put his concern into action.

She lifted her head again to give him a faintly wavering smile. 'You're amazing; thanks, Jamie. I might take a couple in the interval.'

She had been to the dentist earlier that day to have some work done on a back tooth which had begun aching after she bit on a toasted almond, the decoration on a pastry served to them at dinner at their hotel last night.

Saskia had been kept awake half the night by toothache. The tour operator had made arrangements for her to visit a Venice dentist, and while the others had been taking a gondola tour of the smaller canals in the city Saskia went off to have the offending tooth excavated and filled.

She hated going to the dentist, and particularly hated having a tooth drilled, but anything was better than being kept awake with pain.

'Tell me, why is toothache always worse at night?' she had asked the dentist, who had laughed, then given her an admiring look which dwelt longest on her dark red hair and slim, rounded figure before he explained.

'At night you have nothing to take your mind off it.' He had smiled again. 'Unless you are married!'

Saskia had flushed slightly, and the dentist had jumped to a very false conclusion, saying quickly, 'You are not offended, *signorina*?'

'No,' she had assured him and he had smiled at her again, relieved.

'You speak Italian very well, *signorina*.'

'Thank you, *signore*,' she had gravely answered, not explaining why she spoke his language so fluently. For two years she had been lying to people, and Saskia hated being forced to do it yet could see no way out of it. If she told a single soul the truth she might be putting herself at risk. The only safety lay in living a lie.

'You don't live in Venice?' the dentist had asked and she had shaken her head.

'I'm only here for a few days.'

'You must go to the opera while you are here; there is a wonderful new singer at the Fenice this season,' he had told her, his face lighting up with the excitement of the enthusiast.

'Yes, we are being taken there tonight!'

'Ah, *La Traviata* is playing at the moment; you're so lucky to see it in the Fenice—that is where the opera was first performed, you know! Verdi wrote it especially for the Fenice, but the audience didn't like it; it wasn't a success, at first, not in Venice. But the Fenice is the most beautiful theatre in the world. Seventeenth-century, originally, although it was burnt down and rebuilt early in the nineteenth—even London does not have a theatre that old!'

'Covent Garden Opera House is very old, too,' Saskia had mildly suggested, but he had made a disparaging noise, shaking his head.

'Much too big, too ornate and pompous. I don't like those huge theatres. The Fenice is small, intimate, elegant.'

Looking around the theatre when they arrived Saskia had had to admit that his enthusiasm was understandable; the décor of the theatre was delightful, and as always with theatres of that period glittered with gilt and was swagged with elaborate stucco, the ceiling full of cherubs flying from all corners.

When the injection the dentist had given her had worn off the tooth had begun to ache again, but she had taken some pain-killers and the pain had ebbed away gradually during the afternoon. She had almost forgotten about the tooth until Jamie mentioned it, but now that she had thought of it again she felt it give a dull throb.

Pain was like that. If you ignored it, it often went away, but the minute you thought about it again, back it came.

She had been able to forget about Domenico for hours on end over the last few months. Now the pain was back; far worse than toothache and far harder to cure.

The audience around her were humming along with one of the better known arias being performed on stage at that moment. Italian audiences knew all the words and loved to join in with the performers, especially when a famous song had a good tune to it, and celebrated having a good time: wine, women and song. Saskia stared at the vivid party scene on stage, dancers whirling around, people raising champagne glasses to each other, but her mind was elsewhere.

It hadn't once occurred to her that Domenico might be here tonight or she would never have taken the risk of booking for the opera; in fact, she would never have come to Venice at all if she had even dreamt that she might see him there.

Domenico was passionately fond of opera, of course, and went to La Scala, in Milan, frequently. He would never miss any performance of *La Traviata* there, especially by a soprano as fine as the woman singing the heroine, Violetta, tonight, but she never remembered him visiting Venice.

Apart from going to the opera, or to concerts, Domenico was engrossed in his work. He often went abroad, to America, or other parts of Europe, he visited other parts of Italy, and when he was at home he occasionally gave dinner parties, and went to them, but they usually had some business connection. Everything in his life had to fit in with his business.

'I have no time for inessentials,' he had often told her impatiently, when she tried to persuade him to take her to see a light-hearted film or play, or take a holiday in the sun somewhere.

She had often had a secret feeling that he saw her as inessential; a frivolity, a toy he had picked up in an idle moment and enjoyed playing with, but did not actually need.

Domenico had been essential to her; or, at least, she hadn't been able to imagine life without him at one time. It was only when the pain hurt too much that she had fled. There was a limit to love, she had finally been forced to realise, or rather, a limit to how much you could bear in the name of love.

She hadn't seen him since the night she left his house; she feverishly ached to see him now, and at the same time was terrified.

Where was he sitting? Not close to her, she was sure of that, but within sight of her, because he had seen her, before the lights went down.

There was no point in looking around, trying to see him in the darkened theatre. It was full; not a seat vacant in the house, which, the tour operator had told them, was normal for the Fenice. The Venetians loved opera. This particular production had been a runaway success as soon as it opened. The new soprano had a miraculous voice and was lovely to look at, too: black-eyed, with long, silky black hair, worn dressed up in the party scene, but loose and flowing when she was in her bedroom. Her voice had sensuality and so did her slim, sexy body and she had a way of walking across the stage that made every man in the opera house catch his breath and sigh. You couldn't get a seat for months ahead, the tour operator had also told them, pleased with himself for having booked ahead long ago.

'How's the tooth now?' asked Jamie.

Behind them someone hissed, 'Shh...' in an affronted voice.

Jamie made a rueful face at her and looked back at the stage.

Saskia's eyes wandered restlessly. A sea of faces surrounded them; pale glimmering circles in the gloom, all eyes fixed on the party scene taking place on stage.

Which face belonged to Domenico?

She closed her blue eyes, concentrating on finding out exactly where he was sitting. It didn't always work; so much depended on the other person giving off strong enough signals.

Slowly she turned her head, like a radar dish, homing in on his emotions. Anger; black and dark red, she could almost see it in the darkness, like a smouldering fire, which was how she found him, knew when she was looking in the right direction.

He was sitting in a box on the left-hand side of the stage.

She opened her eyes and looked that way, saw the silky curtains swagged and held back with tarnished gold tassels, and between them the stark outline of his head, an immediately familiar silhouette.

He was sitting turned towards her, not towards the stage. She couldn't see his face from this distance, but she didn't need to see him. She knew what she would see if the lights came back up again: black hair brushed back from a high, bony forehead, chiselled features, cold grey eyes, a strong jawline and a mouth which was hard and reined in, yet hinted at potential passion. Domenico was not cold in bed; far from it. He was a possessive and demanding lover, but he kept his emotions in one compartment and his working life in another. The two were never allowed to meet.

Tonight, though, his emotions were uppermost; across the theatre she picked up what he was thinking, feeling, and it made her flinch and tremble.

Jamie felt her betraying movement, turned again and looked at her anxiously. 'Is it getting worse?'

Everyone began to applaud at that moment, some of the men actually getting to their feet, calling out the soprano's name and blowing her noisy kisses, throwing her red carnations.

Under cover of the uproar, Saskia whispered, 'Jamie, I think I'm going to have to go—you stay, though; I don't want to spoil the evening for you.'

'I'm sure that if you take a couple of pills they'll help,' he urged.

She risked a quick glance towards the box where Domenico sat. His head was still turned their way. She knew he was watching them. He couldn't see their faces or hear what they were saying, but if she got up to leave Domenico would follow her, catch up with her.

At the back of the box in which he sat she saw a faint movement, a darker shadow which detached itself as Domenico lifted his hand in a commanding gesture. A man came forward, bent to listen to him.

She drew a sharp breath. The bodyguards. She had forgotten them. He could send them round here to get her! She should run, now.

On the point of getting up she hesitated, biting her lip. Oh, what was the point? If she got away now, he would still be able to trace her through the tour firm. The theatre management would tell him who had booked those seats, and which hotel the tourists were staying at in Venice.

Oh, why didn't I realise how risky this holiday was? she thought grimly. It was crazy to think of coming to Italy, any part of Italy; but after two years she had begun to think there was no need to be so nervous or take elaborate precautions against running into him again.

She didn't know Venice at all, and, remembering that Domenico never went there either, she had decided it would be safe enough, especially as this would be a coach tour, constantly moving on each day until it reached Venice and halted there for a few days. There shouldn't be any risk.

Wrong! she thought, shuddering. She should have stayed in England, in obscurity, where he could never find her. This was his country, his territory; she had made a serious mistake in coming here. Although if she hadn't come to the opera he would never have known she was here, probably.

She wasn't even able to enjoy the opera. She had hardly noticed anything that happened on stage—the girl in the lovely dress whirling around, singing, now that her party guests had gone and she was alone.

Saskia sighed as the girl's singing broke through her own agitated thoughts, and the man beside her looked sharply at her again, leaning over to ask, 'Toothache getting worse?'

She nodded. 'At the end of this act, I'm going, Jamie. You stay, though; I really don't want to ruin your evening.'

'I'll come with you,' he whispered. 'I'm not letting you walk through the city alone, especially when you're not well.'

It was typical of him to insist on that. Jamie Forster was a warm, kind-hearted, friendly man who cared about other people. He wasn't either ambitious or dynamic; all Jamie wanted was to enjoy his life, have plenty of friends, and earn enough to live on, comfortably.

He ran a garden centre, which he had inherited from his late father, in a small country town about forty miles from London. Jamie loved working in the open air, with growing things; he had large but capable and sensitive hands, green fingers, which could make anything grow. He almost casually pushed tiny plants into the earth and they sprang up rapidly, vigorous and hearty. His work was more than a hobby, it was a passion, perhaps his only real passion.

Saskia had grown fond of him since she started working there two years ago, but she had never let him get too close because there was so much she had never told Jamie about her past. She was not free to get involved with anyone. Luckily, although Jamie was clearly fond of her, too, he had never shown any sign of being in love with her. If anything, they were such good friends that anything more intimate was almost out of the question. Jamie had had a girlfriend until a few months ago when they had a big row and broke up because Jamie was more interested in his work than he was in his girlfriend. Now and then he took Saskia with him to parties, but only as a friend; Jamie had never even tried to kiss her.

But would Domenico believe that when he knew that she was on holiday in Italy with Jamie? Saskia bit her lip, her eyes flicking towards where Domenico sat, his head a dark silhouette in the glow from the footlights.

Of course he wouldn't.

He must not meet Jamie. She was terrified of his reaction if he did. Domenico had an ice-cold manner, very controlled, and yet under that ran burning lava which could erupt without warning and devastate those it touched.

Jamie couldn't possibly cope with Domenico in that mood. Nor could Saskia; she never had been able to; he terrified her when the frozen surface of his manner cracked and the fire beneath leapt out.

A moment later, to her relief, the first act finally came to an end. Saskia ruefully clapped with everyone else as the soprano whirled off stage and the curtains closed. She loved *La Traviata*, the romantic, piercingly sweet music and the tragic storyline, the nineteenth-century décor, the wonderful clothes the women wore at that time, the heartbreak of that last act. All day she had been waiting on tenterhooks for this evening.

Yet she hadn't really been aware of anything that was happening on stage!

As the audience began to get up, Saskia ran for the exit, swerving round other people, pushing past anyone who blocked her way, muttering apologies. She didn't look round to check if Jamie was following. She was too busy concentrating on getting out of the theatre before Domenico or one of his bodyguards caught up with her.

She was already a street away before Jamie panted up beside her. 'Hey! You almost lost me! I stopped to explain to Terry that we were going back to the hotel; if he didn't know we had left he would have panicked when he counted up heads and found two missing.'

She gave him an apologetic look. 'Oh, you should have stayed; I'm sorry I've ruined your evening, Jamie! I know how much you were looking forward to *La Traviata*.'

'It isn't your fault; you didn't ask to have toothache tonight!' he said with a resigned sigh. 'It's just fate.'

No, he was wrong, Saskia thought. It wasn't fate that had planned this evening; it was her own stupid folly. If she hadn't come to Italy she would never have been in this theatre, she would never have seen Domenico again.

Yet . . . why had Domenico been there? Had fate been busy, after all?

They came to one of the rounded corners which were so typical of the labyrinthine streets of Venice which curled round and round like the inner spirals of an ear, and Jamie paused, looking up at a street name painted on the wall.

'We go left here, don't we?'

'I can't remember!' Saskia looked around anxiously. She wanted to get as far away from the theatre as possible, quickly. She did not want Domenico to catch up with them.

Venice was such a maze of tiny streets and squares, alleys and canals. She hadn't orientated herself properly yet, and, anyway, had a very poor sense of direction. She could get lost even when she had a map in her hand.

Jamie asked a man walking past and got directions; they started off again and as they approached their hotel at last she began to relax and feel safe. Domenico couldn't catch up with them now.

She knew he had lost them completely. She didn't need to see him to be sure of that. She could feel it; his anger, his frustration, as he realised she had got away again. He was searching the streets around the theatre, she sensed, as if she were watching him; moving with that prowling lope which was characteristic of his tall, loose-limbed, long-legged figure, while his eyes flicked, quick and intent, along alleyways, into empty, moonlit squares, hunting for her.

She knew what he was feeling, although not exactly what he was thinking. Domenico was too clever for her to be able to divine his thoughts. She could only tell what he was thinking when his feelings and his thoughts merged, were one. That rarely happened with Domenico, although with some people it often did.

She had discovered her gift many years ago, when she was a child; she hadn't understood it then, and it was intermittent, so unpredictable, that sometimes months would go by before it happened again, that sudden flash of awareness of what someone else was thinking. Saskia had actually wondered if she was imagining it for a long time, until she reached puberty and it began to happen more frequently. At that age she had experimented with it, turned it almost into a party game for her friends, and been able to check that she was really picking up their thoughts and not imagining them.

Not that she could read everything in their minds, or do so at will, but if ever they were very angry, or upset, or frightened she could tune into those emotions, tell them what they were feeling exactly.

It always amazed them, it even frightened some, who would keep away from her after one such experience, seeing her as someone weird, alarming, even dangerous.

People did not like the idea that you could read their minds and know what they were really thinking, even though she assured them that her glimpses of their minds were fragmentary and arbitrary.

'It's like picking up radio waves,' she had told Domenico once. 'Like voices coming out of the air. I hear what people are thinking... but only if they're very excited or upset; it only happens when there's an extra charge of electricity in their brains, I think, boosting the signals so that I can pick them up. Anger or fear or happiness... I always pick up strong emotions.'

'I can see I'll have to be careful of you,' he had said, those grey eyes of his watching her sardonically, and she hadn't needed to tune into his thoughts to know that he didn't believe her, he thought it was all nonsense, crazy imagination on her part.

Domenico did not believe in other dimensions—in horoscopes or signs of the zodiac, fortune-telling, mind-reading, the tarot, palm-reading or second sight. Saskia didn't believe in most of them, either; she had often tried to explain that she didn't do any of those things, she didn't even pick up other people's thoughts voluntarily any more, she hadn't since her teenage years. She would be glad to stop doing it, especially now, she found it more and more disturbing, but she didn't know how to switch it off or shut it out.

'It just comes,' she had said. 'Out of nowhere, whenever there's a crisis, or someone is really upset.'

Domenico had shaken his head at her, his mouth crooked and incredulous. He hadn't understood or believed a word of what she said; it didn't fit in with his view of the universe or human nature.

He had a clear, diamond-hard, ice-cold mind; logical and rational. Domenico was a perfectionist, about himself, his job, even his life. Even her, she began to realise. Domenico expected her to be perfect, too.

Perfect in looks, in the way she dressed and behaved, in everything she did, the perfect wife for a powerful man like Domenico Alessandros and, he expected, in time, the perfect mother of his no doubt equally perfect children.

Perfection was a hard act to sustain. Saskia was bitterly aware of being human, of failing in some areas of her life, of weaknesses, inadequacies which she could do nothing about, and which, she began to be afraid, Domenico would never forgive in her, when he recognised her imperfection.

He was not a man who forgave easily, and she had failed him. That was why she had run away from him, dreading the icy contempt of his stare, the cutting lance of his voice. She wasn't normally a coward, but Domenico's anger had frightened her; still frightened her.

Two years away from him and yet she still couldn't face him and she knew now, after picking up his feelings across the theatre, that Domenico still hadn't forgiven her, either. His pain and rage were still as bitter.

'You're very quiet—is the pain worse?' asked Jamie anxiously as they collected their keys from the reception clerk and turned towards the hotel lift.

She made a wry, self-mocking face. 'Would you believe ... I've got a headache now, as well?' It was true; her head was thudding as if a little man were perched on top of it banging hammers. She groaned. 'This isn't my day, is it?'

'You must take two of these pills with a glass of water, and then ring Room Service and ask them to bring you some hot chocolate to help you sleep,' Jamie told her, handing her a packet of pain-killers, as the lift slowly moved up to the third floor on which their rooms were situated.

'Thanks, Jamie. I'm sorry...' she began again, and he shook his head at her, smiling.

'Forget it. I've had toothache, I know how you must be feeling. I often think there's no pain worse. My mother often says she'd rather have a baby than toothache any day!'

They walked along the hotel corridor quietly. As they reached her door Jamie paused and looked down at her. 'Now, you get to bed as soon as you've drunk some hot chocolate; and if you don't feel better in the morning we'll make sure you see a doctor, or go back to that dentist and ask him to take another look at your tooth!'

'I'm sure I'll be over the worst tomorrow. I probably just need a good night's sleep. Goodnight, Jamie.'

Saskia didn't bother with hot chocolate; she took the pills and went straight to bed, but although her headache soon died away she couldn't get to sleep for hours. She lay awake in the dark, listening to the soft lapping of water against the piers outside the hotel which fronted the Grand Canal, fighting waves of panic as bad as anything she had felt two years ago.

Then, she had been obsessed with grief and fear and guilt; she had constantly been afraid that Domenico would find her, would track her down and confront her at any minute.

The hard physical exercise of working in the garden centre had helped to get her over those first months. She had not worked so hard for a long time; her muscles had ached heavily in the beginning. She would come in from work, muddy, weary, her skin filmed with sweat, have a long, hot bath in water scented with pine, trying to relax her muscles and ease their aching, and then she would eat a light supper in front of the electric fire before going to bed early. After one of those baths, having been out in the fresh air all day, she would find herself falling asleep the minute her head hit the pillow, and, although at first she had had nightmares every night, slowly over the months those bad dreams had stopped.

She had one tonight, though. Even though she eventually went to sleep, she woke up in the early hours, crying, trembling, and sat up in bed, staring at the paling sky without seeing it, remembering what had happened at the opera last night, wondering if Domenico had discovered that she was one of a group of tourists staying in Venice that week, or if he had believed she was there privately, with the man who had left with her.

For once she wished she could tap into private thoughts at will, but it didn't happen. Her mind was blank. Perhaps Domenico was still asleep? But somehow she knew he wasn't; she felt sure he was awake as well, and that he had had a bad night, too. It was no comfort to be sure of that.

She couldn't stay in her room all day. At seven-thirty, Saskia slid out of bed, went into the bathroom and took a shower, put on a robe just as her breakfast arrived— orange juice, rolls, black-cherry jam, coffee.

She tipped the waiter, who opened the shutters for her, letting in the golden glory of a Venetian morning. When the man had gone, Saskia sat down on her balcony and ate her breakfast, reading the Italian paper which had been sent up on her tray.

She stiffened as she glanced down a business page and Domenico's name leapt out. Hurriedly she read the short item, and understood why he was in Venice. If only she had known! She would never have come here at this precise moment.

Jamie had said to her last night, 'It's just fate,' without realising quite how accurate she was in using those words. Fate had made Jamie suggest a trip to Italian gardens for them both, to get ideas for the garden centre at home; and fate had ordained that that garden trip should end with a few days in Venice before they flew home. Fate had been busy organising Domenico's life, too. He was here, on business; she might have known. Domenico was in the process of negotiating with one of the major Italian hotel chains; he was planning to take over some of their top luxury hotels for his own chain and the chairman of the other company lived here, in Venice, so Domenico had come to Venice.

After breakfast she dressed in a simple apple-green linen dress, slid her feet into flat white shoes, and put on make-up, brushed her hair, before going down to meet up with Jamie and the others on the tour.

This morning they were going back to the Accademia art gallery, which they had already visited once, but which was so crowded with marvellous paintings that they had barely scratched the surface in their earlier visit.

'This time we are going to concentrate on Giovanni Bellini,' their guide told them, and launched into a long talk on the famous Venetian painter. Saskia tried to concentrate on what he was saying, but her mind kept straying back to her own problems. They were here for another two days. Even if she took a plane back to England this morning, Domenico could easily trace her, through the tour operators, get her address and track her down.

What am I going to do? she desperately wondered, following the others out of the hotel on their walk through Venice to the Accademia building.

She hated the thought of running away again, leaving her job, her friends, the little home she had set up over the past two years, having to start again, somewhere else, lying, hiding, maybe even running again at some future time.

Yet was she strong enough, even now, to face Domenico? Her courage failed her at the very idea.

They had been in the Accademia for an hour when Saskia felt that familiar flash inside her brain, as if an electric spark jumped between two points.

She looked hurriedly around, and saw him instantly, at the other end of the room, a tall, lean figure dressed casually, in shades of brown: chocolate-brown brushed-cotton jeans, a matching brown cashmere polo-neck sweater, and worn over that a golden-tan brushed-suede waistcoat under a dark brown leather flying jacket. It all looked haphazard, thrown on in a moment's whim, but Saskia knew Domenico was dressed by the best Italian designers; someone had put that look together, charging an arm and a leg for doing so!

He wasn't looking at her, he was standing in front of a painting by Bellini which Saskia's group had seen earlier: *The Virgin and Child in the Garden*. Domenico was staring fixedly at the mother and child, and the pain in his mind made tears sting under her lids.

She hadn't paused in front of the altarpiece while the tour director was talking about it, she had walked on to the next picture. She hated to see paintings of mothers and babies. She hated even more to feel the anguish Domenico was feeling; it brought back her own, welling up inside her like an inexhaustible fount of tears.

She couldn't bear it. Deliberately she wrenched herself away from those memories, and began to hurry towards the door. He hadn't seen her yet; she could escape before he did.

But even while she skimmed a circuit of the room, avoiding him, she couldn't stop watching him, remembering the tanned and powerful body under his casually elegant clothes, her mouth drying in helpless sensuality. It seemed an eternity since she had touched him, seen him naked, held him in her arms. She would have died to have him just once more.

She was almost at the door, almost out of sight of him, when Domenico's head turned abruptly, as if a string had jerked it round.

He swung, his eyes leaping straight towards her, and she froze in mid-step, staring back, intensely shocked, hearing her heart thudding, her blood running, her body vibrating in response to a realisation that stunned her.

Domenico hadn't known she was there behind him. He hadn't seen her or heard her until now; it had not been one of his five senses that told him she was in the room and it wasn't simply that he had suddenly sensed she was there.

No. It had never happened before, but just now, for the first time, Domenico had picked up her thoughts, her feelings, as she had so often picked up his. He had felt the passion with which she was watching him, even though he hadn't known she was there, behind him, and across the room she felt the heat of his answering desire, like flames leaping out when you opened a furnace door.

CHAPTER TWO

SHE didn't dare think about it too closely. Not now. Like a rabbit Saskia turned tail again to flee, but once more Domenico read her mind and anticipated the move. She hadn't taken more than two steps when he caught hold of her.

'Don't...' The word broke out of her in a hoarse whisper. She couldn't think clearly. There was only that one simple thought in her head. Don't! Behind it pressed all the pain and regret of the past, too complex to be put into words—language couldn't contain it all, or her mind was too clouded and confused by misery to use any words that might express how she felt.

'Don't?' he repeated in that deep, harsh tone which was so familiar although she hadn't heard it for two years. 'Don't what, Saskia? Don't ask you any questions? Don't demand explanations? Don't reproach you? Don't be angry? Don't come too close to you? What mustn't I do, exactly?'

All of that, she thought, unable to look away from him and unable to answer, either.

'Well, say something!' he snarled, bending towards her, and she flinched away. Domenico observed that instinctive recoil, his frown deepening. 'And stop jumping like that. What are you afraid I might do? Hit you? I don't hit women, even if they deserve it, so you can stop pretending to be afraid of me.'

'I'm not pretending!'

The reply was barely audible. He read the movement of her mouth, rather than heard the words, and his own mouth twisted in a cynical smile.

23

'Good; it wouldn't be wise. I think I'll always know now when you are lying to me.'

Her blue eyes watched him wryly. 'You always told me I was crazy, believing in any of that stuff!'

He grimaced. 'Ah, but I'm a little crazy myself, these days, thanks to you.'

'I'm sorry, Domenico——' she began, and he interrupted in a savage voice that made her nerves crackle like fireworks.

'Sorry! My God! Is that all you can say?'

Everyone in the room heard him; Saskia glanced anxiously around but the woman in widow's black, the clergyman, the student in jeans, with long, untidy hair, and the two men in dark jackets with the watchful, hard faces of detectives, who were witnesses and who stared back at her, were all strangers, none of them belonged to her tour.

Where had the others gone? In the silence that followed Domenico's outburst she heard the tour guide talking from the connecting room; he must have led the others in there while she was absorbed in watching Domenico. His voice floated clearly out to her.

'Bellini was strongly influenced by Mantegna, who painted a little picture of St George, the patron saint of England, which we'll find in the next room we visit. Come along, everyone—we must press on!'

Saskia looked pleadingly at Domenico. 'I can't talk here; my friends will come looking for me any minute. I'm not alone, I'm with a party.'

His face darkened with hostility, his voice hard. 'I know, I saw them last night. You realised I'd seen you last night, didn't you?' He paused, staring down into her blue eyes, their dark centres enlarged and glazed with tension. Domenico nodded. 'Yes, don't bother to lie. You knew I was there; I felt your reaction. I knew you were going to run away again.'

She angrily glanced at the two bodyguards lurking near the door, still watching them. 'And I suppose you sent those two to grab me! You still don't go anywhere without them, I notice!'

His eyes hardened. 'I'd be a fool if I did. You know that.'

Yes, she knew. Italy was a dangerous country; anyone with money had to protect themselves day and night.

Quietly, he said, 'Anyway, it was easy to find out that you were part of a group booking and the name of your hotel. I went there this morning, but they claimed not to know where I could find your party. I simply had a gut feeling that I'd find you in the Accademia.'

She drew a sharp breath, turning paler.

So he hadn't known she would be here! He had located her the way she had located him in the theatre last night. A strange, fierce excitement filled her. What did it mean, though? He had never been able to read her mind during the years when they lived together—why now, after two years apart, was he picking up her thoughts and feelings?

Domenico looked away from her, his hard eyes skimming around the room. 'Where are they, anyway?'

'Who?' She was so absorbed in him that she had forgotten everything else and didn't know what he was talking about.

He looked down into her eyes. 'The others in your party.'

'They must have walked into the next room.' It didn't seem to matter; she was too conscious of him for anything else to impinge on her at that moment. Then she frowned, disturbed by how quickly she was being sucked back into that old pattern of fear and helpless response. 'I should catch up with them; they'll wonder where I've got to.'

Domenico's hand shot out, gripped her arm. 'You don't imagine I'm going to let you walk off again, now that I've found you?' His voice was low, almost a whisper, but it had a harsh vibration that made her tremble.

She saw the two bodyguards tense, move closer, watching. Angrily she muttered, 'Let go, Domenico! Do I have to scream the place down?'

A couple moved behind them to stare at a mediaeval fresco, standing far too close for Domenico to risk a public struggle. He had to let her go but his eyes were a threat; she couldn't look away from the darkness in them.

'Who is he?' he muttered through almost closed lips and she tensed, jumping.

'What?' She was playing for time, knowing who he meant and wondering what she should tell him about Jamie.

'I'll find out so you might as well tell me! He's here in the gallery, I suppose? If you won't tell me, I can always ask him. Does he know about me?' He watched her eyes, smiled coldly. 'No, I had a shrewd idea he didn't! What does he know about you? You must have told him something, and from that look on your face I suppose you invented a new past for yourself. He's going to get a shock, then, isn't he, when he is told?'

'Stop it!' she whispered, on the verge of tears. He was right, of course. Ever since she'd seen him in the theatre the night before she had known she was going to have to tell Jamie the truth about herself, and she knew it would be a shock to him to discover how much she had lied.

Domenico's mouth curled like a whip; punitive, unrelenting. 'Are you living with him? Have you been with him ever since you left me?'

Each question was like a blow across the face, his voice was so bitter and hostile. Saskia couldn't bear it.

'No, I'm not living with him, I just work for him!' Her voice shook and the tears threatened to erupt at any minute. 'We're friends, that's all!'

'Friends?' he repeated and laughed shortly. 'You expect me to believe that? When you're here on holiday with him?'

'It's...a sort of working holiday...' she desperately insisted. 'He's my boss; he has a garden centre and I work there. He belongs to a professional association which arranges tours of famous gardens, sometimes in England, sometimes abroad. He knew I hadn't had a proper holiday since I started working for him, so, as he was coming on this trip, he suggested I come along as well. He's very friendly; he likes having company.'

Domenico's eyes glittered like black ice. 'And he hoped to get you into bed while you were in a holiday mood!' he sneered.

Tensely she shook her head at him, willing him to believe her. She was afraid of what he might say or do to Jamie; she had to make him accept that Jamie was not her lover.

'Please believe me, Domenico, Jamie isn't interested in me that way.'

He did not look convinced. 'That isn't the impression I got, and it isn't the impression the people at the hotel had. They seemed convinced that he was your lover.'

Appalled, she asked, 'You questioned the people at the hotel? What did you say to them?' Anything he had said to the receptionist would be sure to get back to the tour guide, who might well repeat it to the other members of the group. People always talked. They all knew she was with Jamie; if Domenico had told the hotel that he was her husband that fact would certainly be passed on, and someone might say something to Jamie before she had a chance to explain everything.

Domenico gave her a dry, cynical glance. 'You're worried about what he may think, aren't you?' She kept forgetting that he somehow seemed able to pick up on her thoughts, and started, her blue eyes flying wide again. Before she could answer his question, Domenico coldly added, 'Don't worry, I didn't tell them anything. I simply checked that you were staying at the hotel, which was when they told me you were there with your boyfriend on a touring holiday. I asked where I could find you, and was told the Garden Tours group were already out, and wouldn't be back until later in the day. Late afternoon, probably, they said.'

Relieved, she let out a sighing breath and nodded. 'Yes, after we have spent the morning in this gallery, we're having lunch at a local trattoria.'

'What about dinner? Have they also made arrangements for this evening, or are you free?' His eyes were hard, intent. 'We're going to talk, Saskia, sooner or later; you might as well get it over with.'

She had faced that now. There was no escape, unless she ran again, and she couldn't bear the prospect of living the rest of her life as a fugitive. The last two years had been full of such tension and nagging dread; she didn't want to live like that for ever. She would have to talk to him. She must make him see that their marriage was over.

Flatly, she said, 'Very well—but not at the hotel. I'll meet you somewhere...tomorrow morning? We have the morning free. I could get away, meet you for coffee at Florian's?'

Florian's was a tourist institution, the most famous café in Venice, with cloudy mirrors and unhurried waiters, on the opposite side of the Piazzo San Marco; it would be crowded with people, with young lovers whispering to each other, with friends, laughing, arguing, flirting, with tourists staring wide-eyed at the cheerful life of the loveliest city in the world, and nobody would notice two apparent strangers sharing a table and talking in low voices. It would be far less conspicuous than meeting somewhere more private, where someone would be bound to notice them together.

Domenico watched her, frowning. 'Very well,' he clipped out. 'Ten-thirty? How much longer are you going to be in Venice?'

'Another two days.' She looked over her shoulder, hearing hurried footsteps approaching, recognising them. Jamie was coming to look for her. 'I've got to go—I'll see you at Florian's at ten-thirty.'

She almost ran, praying that Domenico would not follow her. She and Jamie collided just inside the next room.

'Oh, there you are!' he said. 'I was coming to look for you. What on earth have you been doing? Your tooth isn't playing up again, is it?'

'No, I was looking at the pictures, daydreaming.' She tensed as Domenico strolled past them; she felt his lightning glance as he skimmed a look over Jamie. Saskia couldn't breathe. What if he stopped and said something? She was terrified he would; she felt his anger like a physical blow, brooding, heavy with threat; but he walked away without a word and vanished towards the exit.

Weak at the knees, Saskia said to Jamie, 'I want to get out of here, I've seen enough paintings to last me for a year.'

He laughed. 'I know how you feel. My calf muscles ache—all this walking and standing about looking at paintings is getting a bit much. Why don't we sneak off and have a coffee and sit at a café table out in the sun for half an hour, then take a stroll to the trattoria, to meet the rest of them for lunch?'

'We ought to tell them we're going, or they'll be anxious about us.'

'OK, make your way out of here and wait for me, while I run and tell them what we're doing.'

Saskia wandered out into the sunshine. She looked around warily, but Domenico wasn't in sight, and a few moments later Jamie ran out of the Accademia. They made for a café they had visited before, bought postcards and sat out in the sun, writing messages for friends back in England. Jamie sent one to his parents, another to his sister. Saskia had no family now; her mother had died three years ago, her father some time before that, and she had been an only child. Her closest relative was an aunt in Scotland but they had been out of touch for years. Saskia sent cards to the others working at the garden centre, a friend she played squash with once a week, a struggling young actress who lived in the flat next to hers.

At twelve-thirty they met the others in the trattoria, on a pleasant, sunny side canal leading into the Grand Canal eventually. The meal had been arranged in advance by the tour company. She suspected it was the same one every tour was offered here, but it was very good. They began with *brodetto*, a local fish soup which was cooked all together but served separately yet at the same time; first the broth itself, made with tomato and garlic, in one dish, and in another the fish, clams and squid which had been cooked in the liquid. Along the centre of the table the waiter put down wicker baskets of thick-sliced, golden-crusted Italian bread. Everyone enjoyed this first course, and it was followed by a selection of huge pizzas, from which they could cut themselves whatever they liked: the toppings varied, from simple cheese and tomato with onion, to seafood or chunks of local spicy sausage and garlic. For dessert they were offered ice-cream.

Saskia skipped dessert and just had strong black espresso coffee made in a gleaming chrome machine on the counter of the trattoria.

After lunch the guide told them they could have the rest of the afternoon free. Jamie fanned himself with his straw hat, yawning widely, and decided that what he needed was a siesta in his hotel room.

'I shall do some shopping,' Saskia said.

'Well, be careful; don't talk to strange men!'

She said wryly, 'I won't.' She was always far too cautious to talk to strange men, and today she didn't want to talk to anyone, even Jamie. She needed time alone, to think. 'See you later, Jamie; enjoy your siesta,' she said.

She walked away slowly as if to make for one of the main shopping areas of Venice, but once she was out of sight she doubled back, to wander along the quiet lessused canals, over bridges, through squares, watching the afternoon sun glinting on the ever-present water which made this city so magical. Sunlight gleamed everywhere, on the worn stone of ancient palaces, on geraniums on ironwork balconies, on washing hanging between houses high above alleys, above the narrow canals. She heard the dying echoes of voices along the water, from the backs of crumbling houses, the sound of children laughing, water rippling, women gossiping on their doorsteps, pigeons flapping in the sunny air.

It was a peaceful afternoon, yet she continually had the feeling she was being watched or followed, and kept pausing to look back, her nerves prickling.

There was never anyone there, except Venetians busy about their own lives, shopping, talking, unloading boats on to a quayside, washing windows, watering flowers. None of them ever looked her way.

Saskia walked on each time, trying to shake off her jumpiness, intent on absorbing Venice through every pore. She felt she was learning more about the city this way than in all the sightseeing their guide had been getting them to do.

She got back to the hotel eventually at about five when the sun was beginning to go down and the spring afternoon had cooled.

She felt as if she had been far away, her nerves were quiet, her mind tranquil, but as she crossed the marble floor towards the reception desk she stopped in shock, hearing a voice from a salon leading off the foyer.

Domenico!

What was he doing here? He knew she didn't want anyone on the tour to know about their old relationship; he had agreed to wait until tomorrow to talk, at Florian's. So why was he here now?

She slowly walked towards the open door of the salon, halted on the threshold, stricken at what she saw.

There were only two men in the room, standing by the window, deep in conversation. One was Domenico. The other was Jamie.

She must have made a sound, the merest inhalation, because they both looked round at the same instant.

Saskia had lost every trace of colour. She was white, her blue eyes wide and dark.

Domenico stared back at her, his face coolly expressionless. Jamie, though, was flushed and bright-eyed, and broke out immediately, 'There you are, Saskia! I was just talking about you. Signor Alessandros, this is my assistant, Saskia Newlyn; she is the design wizard. I'm sure she'll be fascinated to see your gardens and will come up with exactly what you want.'

Saskia was dumb, her eyes held by Domenico's, hearing what Jamie was saying without understanding a word of it. What was he talking about?

'Saskia, this is Signor Alessandros...' Jamie said, coming towards her, and Domenico moved beside him, like a hunting animal, light on his feet, yet tense, his body poised to leap for the kill.

Still holding her eyes, he proffered his hand and she automatically put out her own. The first touch of his flesh sent a shiver through her; his skin was cool, his grip powerful. Possessive, she thought. His fingers swallowed her small hand; she felt she would never escape again. She pulled her fingers free in witless panic; for a second he resisted, as if to underline his capacity to take and keep her, then he slowly let her go.

Jamie was quite unaware of any atmosphere between them; he was too excited.

'Signor Alessandros and I got into conversation out on the terrace, Saskia, while I was having some tea. He noticed me leafing through that book on Italian gardens we bought before we came to Italy, and told me it wasn't always accurate. Well, we noticed that ourselves, once we saw some of the gardens, didn't we? The book's full of stupid mistakes; I started to wonder if the guy had actually been to half the gardens.' Jamie laughed, pausing, and, realising that he was waiting for her to agree, Saskia blindly nodded and forced a smile.

'Yes, I remember.' At that moment she didn't; she couldn't think, let alone remember. Her whole body was still shuddering from the effect of touching Domenico again.

'The book is out of date, I think that's the problem,' Domenico said in his deep, husky voice and her body vibrated to the sound. He was watching her, not looking at Jamie; he knew what was happening inside her. 'It was first published years ago,' he drawled, 'but it must be popular because they keep bringing it out again, and some of the descriptions are no longer accurate.'

'A lot of them!' nodded Jamie.

Saskia couldn't take her eyes from Domenico. Earlier that day, in the Accademia's low lighting, she had thought he was unchanged, exactly the same, but the more she looked at him, the more she realised that wasn't true.

His face was thinner, his body leaner; he had visibly lost weight. He had always looked tough; now his olive, tanned skin was drawn tightly over his cheekbones, his face all angles, hard and austere, his grey eyes glittering like razors.

'I explained to Signor Alessandros that I had a garden centre back home in England, and you worked for me,' Jamie said. 'Which was why we took a professional interest in the gardens we'd seen on this trip, and I told him we wished we could have seen some of the gardens of the villas along the Brenta canal.'

Saskia vaguely remembered Jamie talking about the Brenta canal. It was an ancient canal, he had said, on the mainland of Italy, which started somewhere opposite Venice, and flowed inland in the direction of Padua, but she couldn't quite remember why Jamie had been so keen to visit it, nor did she understand why he had talked to Domenico about it.

'But of course there hasn't been time,' Jamie added. 'As we're only here for two weeks, we only just had time for a few days in Venice before we went back, I told him.' He gave her an excited smile. 'And then guess what? Signor Alessandros told me that he actually owned a sixteenth-century villa on the Brenta canal, Saskia!'

Saskia was startled into a gasp, her eyes widening. Domenico actually lived just outside Venice now? Had he sold the house near Milan? When had he moved here?

Their eyes met. 'I haven't owned it for long,' he said, watching her remorselessly, reading her thoughts and answering them. 'I inherited it from a great-uncle a year ago.'

'And guess who designed it?' Jamie burst out eagerly; he didn't wait for her to guess, which was just as well as she wasn't even capable of thinking about it, let alone remembering the names of Venetian architects. 'Palladio!' he said, his face lit up.

During their exploration of Venice he had become a big fan of the Italian architect whose neo-classical styles had influenced architecture all over Europe, including some of the most famous buildings in England. Nothing they had ever seen at home, though, she had decided, could match the beauty of the churches of Venice which

Palladio had designed. The grave classical style he used was given an extra dimension of beauty by the water running beside the churches day and night, reflecting the white stone, the pediments and columns, the measured elegance of proportion, by sun or moonlight.

Saskia was startled. 'Palladio!' The villa must be worth a fortune, then, although that in itself did not surprise her.

Domenico's family were incredibly wealthy; they headed a conglomerate which owned various companies: food-manufacturing, paper-milling, a drug company, a hotel chain. They were hard-working, ambitious, clever men, the men of the Alessandros clan, but they had not got rich suddenly—the family was a very old one; you could trace the name back to the fifteenth century and beyond. They had begun as merchants, acquired land and castles, married the daughters of the nobility. Domenico's father was the head of the clan, and intended that Domenico should take his place in time.

Old Giovanni Alessandros had been obsessed with his family's pedigree, their place in Italian history, their future influence; it was his driving passion. Arrogant, proud, domineering, he had had his own ideas of the sort of woman his son should marry, and when Domenico had first brought her home his father had made it clear that he disapproved of her, resented her, despised her. She simply wasn't good enough for his son. In time he had come to hate her. In fact, he had been one of the main reasons why she had fled two years ago.

Coolly, Domenico said, 'It's a national treasure, one of the few private commissions Palladio fulfilled, but the house is in a bad way. My uncle was a miser, obsessed with not spending money. He hadn't had any work done on the place in half a century; he didn't so much live in it as squat in it, with a couple of old servants who barely did a stroke of work. There's a lot to be done, including work on the gardens, which are a mess, but which I plan to restore to their original design.'

'And he's thinking of adding a classic English-style rose-garden, he loves roses,' Jamie said in a rush. 'Even more exciting, he might consider letting us design it for him, and supply all the roses, Saskia, if you can come up with a design he likes!'

Stiffening, she looked at Domenico. What was all this? What lies had he been telling Jamie? What was he up to?

He smiled at her lazily, narrow-eyed, watchful. 'I gather your tour ends in two days so there isn't much time if you are to come and look round my gardens; you'll have to come tomorrow,' he drawled, and watched her face tighten with comprehension.

So that was it. He was using Jamie to get her to visit his new house? He could think again; she wasn't going within miles of the place.

'There's nothing important on the schedule for to-morrow, is there, Saskia?' burbled Jamie. 'Just a trip out to Murano—we can skip that.'

'I want to see Murano, actually; I was looking forward to that visit,' she stubbornly said, without taking her eyes from Domenico's face, sending him the message she wanted him to get. He might have waited until they had had that talk over coffee at Florian's, he might have given her a chance to explain why she had gone, why she wasn't coming back.

Jamie looked amazed, frowning at her. 'Oh, we can fit in a trip to Murano as well before we go, on our own— we don't have to go with the group—and this is such a wonderful opportunity, Saskia, something we couldn't have hoped for, a visit to one of the private villas along the Brenta, especially one designed by Palladio. It's manna from heaven, as far as I'm concerned. I can't wait. But you must come too; you're the rose expert; we'll need you there.'

Domenico smiled drily at her. 'Yes, you must come, Saskia; I insist that you do,' he murmured, and she tried to read his secret thoughts, to penetrate the bland exterior he was showing her and find out what he was really planning, but she couldn't.

She had never been able to read his mind at will, of course; she never knew when she would pick up his thoughts or feelings; the flashes only came in moments of stress or intense emotion. But this time she sensed something different, something new. Domenico was shutting her out deliberately; his mind was like the blank screen of a computer; she felt no impulses at all coming from him and she had never met that before.

Until now, even when she couldn't read his mind she had always felt the energy of his thoughts, like the hum of an electric machine.

Now there was nothing, no buzz of activity at all, as if his mind had been switched off.

That wasn't possible, of course. His mind was operating all the time. She looked into his hard grey eyes and saw amusement, mockery there, and was startled by that, too. This mood of his was puzzling; at the opera last night she had sensed rage, hostility; this was very different.

It hadn't occurred to her until now that Domenico might have changed inwardly as well as outwardly, but she saw now that he had. His mind as well as his body was different, and not in some small way—he had changed radically; he was not the same man she had left two years ago.

'The easiest way to get there is for me to pick you up in my motorboat,' he said to Jamie. 'What time do you get up? Can you get up early, have breakfast at seven-thirty? Would eight-thirty be too early for me to pick you up?'

'No, that's fine,' Jamie quickly said before Saskia could argue any more, and Domenico gave a satisfied nod.

'Good. Then until tomorrow—I'll see you both on the quay, outside the hotel. Oh, and bring raincoats—the weather forecast is for spring showers—and some strong walking shoes, if you haven't got boots with you—the gardens are large and some of the older paths are overgrown with grass, and can be muddy.'

Jamie gave him a complacent look. 'We did bring boots, actually, because we thought we might need them for some of the bigger gardens, and the tour people warned us that Venice gets lots of rain and some parts of it flood.'

'That's very true—the Piazza San Marco is often under water; that's why the duckboards are often out in the square, and even San Marco itself can be flooded, unfortunately, at certain times. You've been very lucky with the weather so far—we've had fine weather for the past week—but it is about to change, I'm afraid. Spring is always unsettled here.'

'It's just as unsettled back home in the spring!' grinned Jamie, and Domenico nodded.

'I know.'

'You've been to England?' Jamie was interested; it was obvious that he was very curious about Domenico, and Saskia was nervous of that curiosity, it might make Jamie far more observant than usual.

'Many times,' Domenico said. 'Especially lately; I've been going there often over the past couple of years.'

Saskia tensed again, and he looked into her eyes, his mouth twisting with cynical derision.

'I suppose you have business interests there?' asked Jamie, quite unaware of any undercurrents.

'I do, but my visits were mainly personal,' Domenico said, still watching Saskia.

He had been looking for her. She had always known he would; he wasn't a man to give up anything easily. At times over the past two years she had been tensely aware of Domenico brooding over her; she had even felt sure he was in her own country, looking for her, and she had been on tenterhooks until she sensed that he had gone back to Italy again.

She couldn't stand any more. Huskily, she said, 'I've got to go upstairs to change for dinner—excuse me.'

'See you later,' Jamie said as she retreated.

'See you tomorrow,' Domenico said, with a silky threat hidden in his smooth tone.

Safely in her room, she went into the bathroom and ran a bath, took off her apple-green linen dress, was about to take off her slip when she heard a sound in her bedroom. She ran back in there, her nerves thudding as she saw Domenico closing the door.

'How did you get in here? What the ...?'

He leaned his broad shoulders on the door in a cool pose, smiling mockingly. 'I told the floor maid I'd forgotten my key and my wife was in the shower and hadn't heard me knocking, and she let me in with her pass key.'

'She must have realised you weren't part of our group! She can't have believed you were with me; this is a single room!'

'She must have forgotten that. She was a charming girl, and very helpful; I gave her a handsome tip.'

Saskia shook with anger. 'You mean you bribed her to let you in here! My God, I'll call the manager!'

'And lose the girl her job?'

'Someone that untrustworthy shouldn't be working in a good hotel. She could be letting thieves into rooms, if she let you in here!'

He didn't seem to be listening; he was too busy staring, his grey eyes intent on her naked shoulders and half-covered breasts, the way the silky slip clung to waist and hip, a wide hem of lace ending mid-thigh.

In a mirror on the wardrobe behind him Saskia caught sight of herself and was shocked to realise that with the sun streaming through the window behind her the slip was totally transparent. She might as well have been naked from her waist down, the flat stomach, rounded hips, the dark triangle of hair and below.

Saskia suddenly couldn't breathe. She backed away, watching him with her heart knocking in her throat, her hand going out to catch hold of a white towelling robe on the end of the bed.

Domenico moved faster, caught hold of her, his hands splayed across her smooth, bare shoulders.

'No!' she cried out in panic, but her body was burning, aching, and his body moved against her, one hand sliding down her back to push her closer until they were touching. She trembled, mouth dry, perspiration prickling on her skin.

The conflict between wanting him and being afraid of the pain of loving him made her almost helpless. She had escaped this trap before; now she was back in it again, betrayed by her own desire, weak in the face of his.

Domenico's mouth hunted for hers; she evaded it, turning her head from side to side. He bent his head and she gasped as his lips brushed her shoulder, crept along the collarbone to her neck, pressed deep into the soft skin. One hand caressed her back, followed the deep indentation of her spine, the other hand moved up to her breast and cupped the full, warm flesh.

She gave a smothered moan and wrenched herself free, retreated to the door, opened it before he could get to her.

'Do I have to scream, or will you leave quietly?'

Darkly flushed, breathing audibly, Domenico sat down on her bed. 'OK, you win—I'll go in a minute; I just want a word with you first.'

She didn't lock the door again, she held it almost shut, watching him warily.

'Well?'

'I want to make sure you aren't going to bolt for it again, because I'm having the hotel watched, you wouldn't get far, so don't bother to try it.' He gave her a dry smile. 'I just thought I'd save you the trouble and embarrassment of attempting to get away and being caught.'

She wasn't surprised, but the threat made her angrier. 'Go away,' she said, opening the door wide.

'And I would have to break the news to your friend Jamie that you're my wife, wouldn't I?' he murmured, then got up, walked past her, his eyes on her every step of the way, making her body shudder.

She slammed the door shut on him, shaking so much that she sank down on the floor, her eyes shut, rocking herself like a distraught child, dry sobs in her chest.

Her bath was cold when she remembered it. She had to run some more hot water into it to make it bearable. She only spent a short time in the lukewarm water, towelled herself and put on her robe, lay down on her bed, trying desperately to think.

She had to confess the truth to Jamie, and she knew he would be sympathetic; he'd understand why she had fled, why she had lived a lie for two years. But she still couldn't bear the thought of talking about it. The past was an unhealed wound; it would hurt too much to tell Jamie about it.

But what was she going to do about tomorrow? Be on the quay with Jamie, let Domenico take her to this Palladian villa he had inherited? But would he ever let her leave again?

Her only chance was to stick to Jamie like glue while they were at the villa. Whatever Domenico tried to do she wouldn't let him separate them, or, at least, she would always keep Jamie in sight and make sure Jamie could see her all the time.

The trouble was, she knew how Jamie could be once he was looking at a strange garden, especially an old garden which would no doubt have some old and possibly forgotten, or rare, species in it; he would be too absorbed in plants and trees to notice what was happening to her.

Another, even more disturbing thought hit her. What if other members of the Alessandros clan were living at the villa? They were such a close family, always visiting each other.

What if his father was there?

Ice trickled down her spine.

She could not face Giovanni Alessandros. The very prospect was a nightmare. Two years ago he had tried to kill her, and she was afraid that if he thought she was coming back into his son's life he might try again.

CHAPTER THREE

JAMIE explained to Terry, the tour organiser, that they would be going off separately next day, taking great pride in explaining where they were going.

Terry frowned at him. He had constantly stressed security while they were travelling around Italy, but since they had reached Venice he had seemed less concerned about that, claiming that Venice had the lowest rate of crime in Italy because criminals found it far too much of a problem to get away after committing a crime. Unlike most cities in the world, Venice suffered from little urban theft; muggers and pickpockets rarely tried their luck. Without roads, they had to rely on boats for an escape, and the police could soon catch up with any boat, however fast, in these waterways. The local police had the advantage of knowing everything there was to know about the local waters, and in such a small city most people knew their neighbours far too well for anyone to get away with a life of crime for long.

Now, though, Terry looked uneasy. 'Sounds a bit fishy to me. What did you say this chap's name is? Did he give you any proof that he owned a Palladian villa on the Brenta? Far-fetched story, isn't it? Have you any idea how much a place like that is worth? He'd have to be as rich as Croesus.'

Jamie looked startled. 'I hadn't thought of that. But come to think of it, he dressed as if he had money. His shoes were handmade, I'm certain of it. I coveted them, anyway, I noticed how good they were, and I know I could never afford to buy shoes like that; they must have cost a fortune.' He made a wry face. 'But then I spend most of my time wearing wellington boots! I take your point, Terry, but I don't think there's much doubt he has money, wouldn't you say so, Saskia?'

She didn't reply, but that didn't matter because it was a purely rhetorical question; Jamie didn't wait for her to say anything, he just went on thoughtfully, 'Although, I have to say, it was odd, getting into conversation with him out on the terrace; I mean, he went out of his way to talk to me.'

'There you are, then!' Terry said, and Jamie looked uncertainly at him.

'I remember now, he came and sat at my table, when there were plenty of other tables free. Mind you, he said it was because he noticed I was reading a book on Italian gardens, and maybe it was. After all, why should he lie to me? What would be in it for him?'

Terry looked pityingly at him, sighed heavily. 'Well, Jamie, I can think of several motives—Venice is the safest city in Europe, but now and then a conman does slip through their net, and if he's talking of taking you off alone with him, in his boat, you could end up anywhere.'

'Oh, that's ridiculous!' Jamie broke out, laughing. 'Why on earth would he want to kidnap me?'

Terry looked at Saskia, his eyes sly. 'Maybe it isn't you he's interested in?'

She went pink, her nerves jumping and her eyes opening wide, startled by his shrewd guesswork.

Jamie looked at her, too, his face changing. 'Saskia? Oh, that hadn't occurred to me. Mind you, I did notice him staring, but...well, that isn't unusual, especially in Italy. Italians always notice pretty women.'

'Italians notice women, period!' Terry said. His eyes slipped down over Saskia again and she quivered with distaste, looking away. She had thought for an instant that he might know something about her and Domenico, but now she saw that that wasn't it at all. Terry had a nasty mind. No Italian had ever looked at her with that expression; their admiration was usually warm and open, it didn't make her feel sick, the way she felt now with Terry staring at her like that.

'You think he's hoping to impress her with his money?' Jamie asked.

'Let's just say I wouldn't trust him,' Terry shrugged. 'After all, a rich man would surely get a local expert to design his rose-garden! Someone from around here would know local conditions better than you could, however good you are, and I'm not being rude, Jamie. Just that a local would know what grows best here, what never thrives, what the weather does at various times of year, and so on, now, wouldn't he?'

Jamie reluctantly had to agree. 'Yes, you're right, I suppose so, but we do specialise in roses, as I told him; we have a huge variety of them in stock, and we do get orders from the continent all the time, especially from France, where they're very fond of English roses even though they grow some marvellous roses themselves.' He frowned, silent for a while, then his face cleared and he burst out, 'No! You know, I do think you're wrong; I don't believe he was just interested in Saskia, because he invited me to see his villa before she arrived! He had never set eyes on her until then.' He beamed at Saskia. 'Mind you, he could be trying to pick our brains without having to pay us a penny. If he takes us round his gardens as tourists we can't charge him for any advice he gets from us. You know how mean people can be about paying for advice! And the richer they are, the more they hate parting with money!'

'Well, I hope you're right,' Terry said flatly, sounding unconvinced. 'In your place, though, I'd think twice about taking him up on his invitation.'

Jamie frowned while he finished his main course, a dish of calf's liver fried with fresh leaves of sage, served with onions.

'That was delicious!' he said to the waiter as the man whisked away his plate, looking cross because Jamie was the last at table to finish that course.

The waiter mumbled a reply and Jamie suddenly did a double take, catching his arm. 'Giorgio! You were serving tea on the terrace this afternoon, weren't you? Did you notice the man who joined me at my table?'

'Signor Alessandros?' The man shrugged. 'Yes, *signor.*'

'You know him?' asked Jamie eagerly.

'But, of course, *signore*—he owns this hotel!' said the waiter, sniffing.

Saskia drew a shaken breath.

Terry sat up in his chair, staring at the waiter. 'Signor Alessandros?'

'He owns the hotel?' repeated Jamie, his face incredulous. 'Are you sure?'

The waiter nodded vehemently. 'Very sure, *signore*. He bought it last year; he lives on the mainland, opposite Venice, in a very beautiful, historic house on the Brenta canal, and is often here, in the hotel. I have served him many times.'

Terry was scowling. 'If you had told me his name was Alessandros, I'd have known who he was,' he said, his face envious and faintly resentful. 'I haven't actually met him myself, but of course I've heard of him—he owns a number of hotels we use, his family own a hotel chain with hotels all over Italy; he must be one of the richest men in the country.'

'Well, I'm relieved to find I was right to trust him!' Jamie said cheerfully, drinking some of his red wine.

'Good heavens, yes,' said Terry, staring at him in a puzzled way. 'You're very lucky to be invited to his home! I can't get over it. You say he just came over and introduced himself? It's amazing. I tell you what, I'll get down early tomorrow morning and see you off, just to check that it is him—I'd know his face anywhere; I've seen pictures of him in Italian papers a hundred times.'

Saskia gave him a dry look. Now that he believed Jamie had really met Domenico, Terry was eager to scrape acquaintance too. She wasn't surprised; she had met that attitude far too many times during the years she'd spent with Domenico. Money had that effect on people; it drew them like a magnet.

Terry caught her cynical glance and went an ugly red. 'Well, time to make my little talk to everyone,' he said hurriedly, getting up. 'I must get my notes for tomorrow, to check our itinerary. Excuse me.'

When he had gone, Jamie grinned at her. 'I think he's jealous; he'd have liked to meet Mr Alessandros.'

'I think you're right,' Saskia said, smiling back at him.

He gave her a sharp, searching look. 'You don't like him, do you, Saskia?'

'Terry?' she asked, opening her eyes wide.

'No, Alessandros,' said Jamie drily. 'I'm not stupid, you know. The minute you walked into that room this afternoon and saw him, you bristled like a cat seeing a dog.'

She had wondered if Jamie would pick up any hint that she knew Domenico. It seemed he had, but wasn't making the right deductions from what he'd seen.

Gently, he said, 'I've always respected your instincts; you've often been proved right about people. So tell me—what don't you like about Alessandros?'

She drew a long breath, wondering if now was the time to tell him the truth, but while she was trying to decide how to begin explaining Terry came back, clapped his hands and asked for silence.

Saskia gave Jamie a shrug, then turned to listen to Terry making a long speech about the wonderful meal they'd just eaten, and he hoped they had enjoyed their day—their second visit to the Accademia had obviously been popular, and hadn't the lunch been good, too?

Everyone clapped, nodding.

Terry gave them an approving smile. 'Now, tomorrow is going to be another long day, as you know. We are going to Murano, on the *vaporetto*, to see the famous Venetian glass being made. The glass factories were set up on Murano in the late thirteenth century and Venetian glass has been much sought after ever since. You will have an opportunity to buy some glass while we are on Murano...'

'I bet we will; he's always taking us off to buy local souvenirs wherever we are—I reckon he gets a cut!' muttered one of the other tour members, and those around him smothered giggles.

The tour guide gave them a cross look. 'Nobody will pressure you into buying anything, but many people do like to buy a souvenir of their visit,' he huffily told them. 'Oh, and I understand several of us won't be coming to Murano, they have made private arrangements—but I would ask them to make sure they are back at the hotel before dinner in order to hear the plans for our last day in Venice.'

They were served their dessert while he talked; it was far too sweet for Saskia, who declined it, but Jamie took a big slice of the meringue ring filled with chestnut purée and whipped cream, and managed to eat all of it. Working in the open air so much gave him a hearty appetite, but Saskia was too upset and worried to want to eat.

Coffee was served while the guide was answering questions about the history of Murano. Saskia pushed her problems aside to listen intently, fascinated by what he was saying and wishing she were going with them. Well, maybe she could squeeze in a private trip on the last day? The trouble was, there was so much to see, so much to do here; there simply wasn't enough time to do everything.

She went to bed early, but didn't sleep well. She had bad dreams all night. She had booked a wake-up call from the hotel operator; when the phone shrilled she jumped up, bleary-eyed, yawning, and fumbled with the receiver.

'Yes? Oh, thank you,' she mumbled, then put the phone down again.

She couldn't have had more than four hours' sleep; she felt terrible but much as she would have loved to she couldn't go back to sleep. Her breakfast would be here soon. Outside she heard the splash of rain and groaned— that was all she needed! Tramping around wild gardens in this weather wasn't going to be much fun.

She showered rapidly, got dressed in suitable clothes for rough walking—fawn cotton jeans, a yellow-striped white shirt and over that a yellow sweater. Blow-drying her auburn hair into its current bell-shaped style, she decided not to put on make-up; she rarely did during the day when she was working in the open air.

Her lined green wax jacket should keep out the rain, and had a hood. She wore flat walking shoes, but would be taking boots with her, in a large duffel bag; she would obviously need them on site in this weather.

She looked at herself in the mirror with satisfaction. She looked sensible, practical, down-to-earth, far from alluring—which was just how she wanted to look today. She wanted to keep Domenico at a distance, not attract him!

There was a tap on her door. 'Room service, *signorina*!'

Breakfast was the usual one: coffee and rolls, black cherry jam, orange juice. She still wasn't hungry, but she forced some of it down, to stop her stomach churning like a washing machine. Nerves were making her feel quite sick.

As she left her room later she walked into Jamie who grinned at her, bright-eyed and full of excitement.

'Good, you're ready! I was just going to knock on your door; we mustn't be late.'

'Have you seen the weather? We're going to get soaked to the skin tramping around these gardens!'

'Rain never bothers you back home!' protested Jamie, who was sensibly dressed for this weather, too, in jeans and boots, a sweater, a dark green wax jacket.

It was true, of course; they worked in all sorts of weather—snowstorms didn't even stop them, although they tended to look for indoor jobs in thunderstorms!

They took the lift down to the ground floor and walked through a corridor to the door leading out on to the paved terrace where tea was served, built out from the hotel's mooring platform on the Grand Canal.

Beside the wooden platform stood several rows of brightly painted striped poles on which boats could tie up, and several bobbed there now: two motorboats painted in the hotel's livery colours, and the other a very much larger sleek motor vessel painted black and white but bearing on the side a coat of arms in a gold shield.

Saskia stiffened, recognising it at once. Jamie wasn't looking at the boat; he was looking at Domenico who was standing on the terrace under a wind-whipped hotel canopy talking to Terry, the tour organiser.

'Creep!' Jamie whispered to her, watching Terry smile and nod eager agreement with whatever Domenico said to him. 'I knew he was hoping to get to talk to Alessandros! Didn't I tell you?'

'I'm sure Mr Alessandros is used to it,' Saskia said, knowing perfectly well that Domenico had met people like Terry all his life and knew precisely how to deal with them: coolly, politely, distantly, never losing his temper or permitting them to gain an inch.

She glanced sideways towards another boat which had tied up near by; a more anonymous-looking boat, black-painted, unmarked. There were two men on the deck, leaning on the roof of the small cabin, and they were staring around them, eyes like lasers, watching everyone outside the hotel, looking up at the windows, at the rooftops, along the Grand Canal, constantly alert for any threat.

Even today Domenico had not left his bodyguards behind, even though they were discreetly watching from a distance.

She felt sick at the thought of why they needed to be there—the ever-present threat of kidnap or assassination for a man as rich and influential as Domenico. What a crazy world this was! How could he bear to live like it? she had often asked him. She had hated living in that world with him; she had often felt like a goldfish in a bowl, swimming round and round with eyes constantly watching her, knowing there was no escape, no hiding place.

At that instant, Domenico turned, as if picking up her thoughts. His grey eyes swept over Saskia, from the dark auburn of her hair to the framed composure of her face, which gave nothing away of how she was feeling, nothing of her anger and pain and fear, then down to the slender figure just as concealed under the neat and sensible, unglamorous, unalluring clothes.

A wry smile twisted his mouth. 'I see you're ready for anything!' he drawled, and she knew there was a secret meaning hidden in the words, but her features didn't betray any expression to let him know that she had understood.

Domenico was dressed casually, too, in a thick black fisherman's sweater and jeans, knee-length black fisherman's boots on his feet. He looked tougher than ever, his olive skin wind-flushed, his dark hair ruffled. She wished he didn't look sexier, too, but her skin prickled with awareness of him and heat burned in the pit of her stomach. Just looking at him turned her on. She only hoped he wasn't picking up the instant leap of desire inside her, the way he had in the Accademia.

'I've been trying to persuade Mr Alessandros to allow the tour company to visit his lovely home one day; I hope you'll say a good word for us while you're there,' Terry told them. He smiled obsequiously at Domenico. 'We are a very select organisation, I assure you; our clients are all highly recommended—they are mostly professional people. You need have no fear of damage being done, and if any accident did occur we carry very good insurance.'

Impatiently, Domenico said, 'You fail to grasp what I keep telling you—my home is private, I do not want strangers invading it!'

Eagerly, Terry said, 'Oh, but the inconvenience would be minimal—we only do these tours around Venice two or three times each year, and we wouldn't stay at the villa for long—two hours, at most——!'

'For the last time, the answer is no!' Domenico interrupted. He began walking towards his boat, saying brusquely over his shoulder to Jamie and Saskia, 'Let's get on our way, shall we?'

Terry caught Jamie's arm and detained him, muttering. 'Try to talk him round, will you? It would be such a feather in my cap if I could add his house to our list of places we visit.'

Domenico jumped down into his boat; he turned to Saskia, silently held out his hands to lift her down.

She hesitated, their eyes met, and she felt colour sweep up her face. Before she could jump down, his hands closed on her waist and she drew a long, shaken breath.

The next second her feet were off the ground and she was floating through the air, down towards him. He didn't hurry to put her down, he let her slide downwards, held very close to him, their bodies actually touching in an intimacy which made her gasp.

She could hear Terry and Jamie talking behind them, and shot a look their way, flushed and startled, but Jamie had his back to her. As her feet touched the boat's deck, she tried to pull free. Domenico's hands tightened. He looked down at her, his face brooding, inches away from hers.

'You look like a boy in those clothes,' he whispered. 'You know I hate to see you wearing trousers.'

'I don't dress for you any more!'

'Or undress for me?'

Her face burned. She could hear the heavy thud of a heart beating much too fast; was it hers, or his?

'Stop it, Domenico!' she muttered.

'Stop what?'

'If you're going to talk like that, I'm going back into the hotel!'

Pointedly, he asked, 'Have you told your boss that you're my wife yet?'

She bit her lip. 'I'm going to!'

'What a coward you are, Saskia!' he observed in a neutral voice.

She went white again. 'Let go of me!' she whispered, hating him.

His voice lowered to a harsh, angry whisper. 'Two years! I haven't seen you for two long years, and you stand there and ask me to let you go? If you think I'm letting you go again when I've only just found you, you're crazy! I've had people combing Britain from one end to the other, I've gone over there myself, whenever one of my detectives thought he might have tracked you down, only to find it was another false trail. Several times I had to go over to see if I could identify a woman fitting your description who had committed suicide...'

She winced, and his eyes lashed her bitterly.

'Yes, it wasn't an experience I want to repeat! If it had been you...' He broke off, his mouth grim. 'It was a hellish experience. You've put me through a nightmare, Saskia, and the worst of it was the uncertainty about what had really happened to you...if you were alive or dead...if you had found someone else...two years of it, Saskia. Seven hundred and eighty-three days, to be precise—I counted every single day, all the frustration and hope and fear...'

'I'm s——' she began and he interrupted in a snarl.

'Don't say you're sorry again!'

She looked up at him with pain and regret in her dilated blue eyes, struggling with tears.

'What else can I say?'

'We used to be able to talk to each other!'

'That was before...' He broke off as a tear escaped and ran down her white cheek. He put a hand out in a quick, involuntary movement, and his fingers brushed her cheek, brushed away the tear. 'Don't cry, I can't bear to see you cry,' he muttered in a low, rough tenderness, his face moving down towards her as if he was going to kiss her, and she arched away from him with a hoarse, anguished cry.

She could not bear the thought of him kissing her.

Domenico's anger returned in a surge like the sea on a stormy day; she felt it beating inside him with all the violence of the elements let loose, and her terror rose to meet it.

They looked at each other in bitter tension, and then their mood was shattered by the sound of Jamie hurrying across the stone terrace.

Domenico let go of her, turned away and went into the cabin of the motor cruiser; she heard him moving about in there while she trembled, and tried to pull herself together.

'Sorry to keep you waiting!' Jamie said, jumping down into the boat, making it rock at its moorings, then he saw that there was only Saskia on board, and he dropped his voice, asking her, 'Where has he gone?'

She couldn't speak, simply gestured towards the cabin, not meeting Jamie's eyes.

'Was he furious over Terry?' whispered Jamie. 'I could see he was getting irritated. I tried to get away, too, but

Terry went on and on; he wants me to talk Alessandros into letting the tour company use his villa! He must be crazy if he thinks Alessandros would even consider it! I only hope he hasn't ruined our own chances!'

Saskia held back a sigh. She shouldn't let Jamie go on hoping that his company were going to get a prestige order out of this trip! Domenico was only using that as bait to get her to the villa, but how could she tell Jamie that without explaining everything?

She was barely able to speak at all at that moment, after that last painful clash between herself and Domenico. She couldn't have told Jamie anything, not now, not yet. If she tried, she knew she would break down. The tears were very close to the surface already; they would spill out if she started talking about the past.

No, she would choose her moment to tell Jamie, when she was alone with him; she certainly wasn't doing it with Domenico within earshot.

The engine fired, they felt the deck rocking under their feet, and then Domenico reappeared, said curtly to Jamie, 'Cast off, will you?'

Jamie sprang to obey; Domenico looked at Saskia, said in the same brusque tone, 'Come into the cabin and sit down; I'm going to be moving quite fast soon, and I don't want you falling overboard or hitting your head on the deck.'

She silently obeyed and a moment later the boat began to surge forward, along the Giudecca canal, heading for the open lagoon. Jamie joined her as they left the shelter of the canal and the boat put on real speed, bouncing over the waves, spume flying, drops dashing against the windows of the cabin.

Jamie had one of his guide books in his pocket; he pulled it out and began to read bits out to her.

'The Brenta canal runs inland from Fusina...we should be there soon at this speed!'

Saskia was looking back at Venice, some distance from them now, sinking into the early morning mist, the domes and cupolas and spires touched with the rising sun. The city had an unearthly beauty which made it dream-like, the colours sharpening with the growing light, pastels which washed down into the water in reflections that swam and dazzled, a gold which repeated the morning sunlight. She wished she had brought a camera with her, but sensed that no photograph could do justice to what the human eye could see with such moving intensity.

Jamie was too busy reading his guide book to notice. '"There are villas along the banks at frequent intervals, built over centuries. From the Renaissance onwards, rich Venetians came out here to escape the heat and sickness of the sweltering summers of the city; for weeks Venice would be deserted, except by the poor..."'

'Who couldn't afford a holiday!' Saskia drily said.

'Well, what's new under the sun?' Jamie said, grimacing. 'Where was I? Oh, yes, "merchants and their wives don't seem to have pursued country pleasures during the early period of the Brenta villas; they went on as they did in town, gambling, dancing, having parties."' Jamie paused and looked up, grinning at her. 'Sounds like fun! But you'd have thought they would prefer to sit out in their gardens!'

'If they did, they wouldn't have done the gardening!' Saskia pointed out. 'They took their servants with them, I expect, and the servants had a working holiday!'

'I expect they enjoyed that better than being left in the city. I know I should have done,' said Jamie, grinning.

'I don't know. If they were left behind they would probably have had less to do.'

'Yes, but listen to this...' Jamie read on relentlessly. '"The canals probably stank during the very hot months, since they were full of sewage and other refuse, and the sirocco, a wind blowing from Africa, and often gritty with dry, hot sand, would have made life oppressive because people couldn't go out of doors while it blew, and even when it was not blowing there would have been hot, sticky, humid days and nights when it was impossible to sleep, not to mention the ever-present threat of typhus from bad water, and malaria, from mosquitoes breeding in stagnant water."'

'Sounds wonderful,' Saskia said with sarcasm and Jamie laughed, pushing his book back into his jacket pocket.

'Well, you can see why they preferred to move out into the country during hot weather!'

'If they could afford it!'

Domenico's pace was slowing now; looking out, she saw they were entering the mouth of the Brenta canal, between rotting piers. The boat seemed to be inching its way along; it seemed safe enough to go out on deck again to get a better view. In front of them she could see the smaller boat carrying the bodyguards.

'Look!' Jamie broke out suddenly and there ahead of them, through a fringe of ancient trees in new leaf, they saw a worn stone portico, with a pediment above, and, supporting it, classical columns, while above rose creamy stone walls broken up by perfectly proportioned windows.

Excited, Jamie looked round at her. 'Do you think that's it?'

As if in answer, the boat slowed even further, nudging in to the green banks. Domenico called out to Jamie, 'Get ready to tie up!'

Saskia stared up at newly rebuilt walls, elaborate iron gates through which a man in a dark jacket stared down at them.

His eyes skated over her, his face expressionless, but she saw him raise a hand in greeting to the two men in the other boat and Jamie gave them a startled look, apparently only just noticing them.

'Who are they?' he thought aloud.

'His bodyguards, Jamie.' Saskia's flat tone caught his attention; he looked at her sharply.

'His bodyguards? Do you think so? Have they been following us ever since we left Venice, then? You never said anything—when did you notice them?' He broke off as the two men jumped off their boat and stood with their backs to the house, watching the canal, the opposite bank, their eyes constantly moving from spot to spot, their bodies tense and alert.

'I spotted them at the hotel,' Saskia said. 'They've been with us all the way.'

'I think you're right,' Jamie whispered, looking both impressed and horrified. 'You don't think...I suppose we're in no danger, here with him? I mean...I wonder if he's expecting to be attacked?'

'They wouldn't be there otherwise, Jamie!'

Saskia felt almost angry with him for being so innocent and naïve, but then hadn't she been as blithely unaware when she first met Domenico? From the ordinary world of people like her and Jamie it was hard to imagine the sort of life a man like Domenico Alessandros led.

Jamie looked nervous now, and Saskia was afraid, too, for different reasons—afraid of what she might find in the villa, of *whom* she might find.

'Tie up now!' yelled Domenico and Jamie leapt on shore.

Saskia began to put on her boots; the path looked muddy. Domenico's shadow was cast by the sun like a black bar across the deck. He stood watching her; without looking at him she huskily asked, 'Is your father here?'

Domenico shot her a narrow-eyed look. She picked up the beat of his thoughts, hard, searching, angry. They made her shiver.

'Why?' he demanded.

She couldn't meet his eyes. 'Is he?' she repeated.

'No.' The word grated.

A quivering sigh escaped her.

Harshly, Domenico burst out, 'What happened that last day, Saskia? My father won't tell me, but I know something happened between the two of you. Was it something he said that drove you away?'

Eyes dark and enormous in her white face, she looked at him and couldn't answer, helplessly shaking her head. How could she tell him when it terrified her to remember, let alone talk about it?

CHAPTER FOUR

'WHY does it frighten you to remember?' Domenico's voice was low and careful, like that of someone trying not to frighten, but it still startled her. She drew a painful breath.

'What?'

'That's what you were thinking, wasn't it? That it frightened you to remember that day.'

'You *are* reading my mind...' she whispered, white as paper, her eyes like black holes.

He moved impatiently. 'God knows what's happening, but now and then I seem to know what you're thinking, maybe because I've spent so much time over the last two years trying to work out exactly what went wrong between us. Saskia, why won't you tell me what happened the day you ran away?'

'Please stop talking about it!' she burst out and looked up the bank. Jamie was staring at them. 'Jamie is watching us; we'd better go!'

Domenico muttered under his breath, something angry and dismissive of Jamie. Turning abruptly, he leapt up on to the bank and turned to offer her his hand to help her up, too.

He didn't let go of her hand at once; he held it, tightly, one thumb slowly caressing her blue-veined wrist, as if feeling the beat of her blood under the skin while he stared down insistently into her wary blue eyes.

'Saskia, we are going to talk while you're here, and we're going to have to get rid of Jamie so that we can have our talk in private. Don't make it difficult for me, by arguing, or trying to keep him around, because if I have to I'll talk in front of him, and it's obvious that you don't want him to know the truth, for reasons I'm not entirely sure I like.' He paused, his face tightening again. 'Are you sure he's just your boss, Saskia? Or is he more than that?'

Saskia felt him trying to read her mind again, felt his concentration bearing down on her, and was both disturbed and angry. She would be afraid to think at all very soon; there was no privacy even inside her own head.

'No, Domenico!' she muttered, making her mind as blank as she could. 'I'm not interested in Jamie, not that way! I'm fond of him and I like him, as a friend, nothing else!'

His smile was coldly derisive. 'A platonic relationship? Between a man and a woman?'

'Don't tell me you don't believe in them, or I might remind you of what you once told me about that secretary of yours!' Her voice was tart, there was a flash of jealousy in her eyes.

His eyes narrowed, intent and bright. 'Claudia? The best secretary I ever had; I've missed her every day since she left.'

'She left? Why?' Saskia was stunned by this news. She had never liked his secretary, whose attitude had been openly hostile from the moment she and Saskia first met. Claudia Forli had been a beautiful, sensual woman in her early thirties, raven-haired, with glossy black eyes and a full, pouting red mouth. She had worked for Domenico for eight years and from the way she looked at him Saskia had been forced to suspect that the two of them had had an affair some time, but Domenico had insisted that they hadn't.

'I was never interested in her that way,' he had said, shrugging, and she had believed him at the time, although she had still been sure that Claudia was in love with him, even if he didn't know it.

Domenico frowned, and suddenly Saskia picked up a new tension in him; there was darkness in his mind, anger.

Startled, she looked at him, trying to work out what was wrong now.

He turned away, saying over his shoulder curtly, 'Oh, she got married.'

'Married?' Saskia followed him up the hill, wondering if Claudia had given up hope that Domenico might ever look her way, and had taken second-best. Plenty of men had pursued Claudia; she would have had no trouble in marrying one of them.

If Domenico was angry, though, it had to mean that he must have cared more for Claudia than he had ever realised. He had admitted that he missed her. Had he...? She felt a chill feather her skin and shuddered in sudden jealousy. Had he had an affair with Claudia after all?

If so, when? Before their marriage? Had he lied to her when he'd claimed that he had never been interested in Claudia that way? Or had the affair happened after their marriage broke up? Had Domenico turned for comfort to Claudia? Could she blame him if he had? she thought wearily.

Domenico glanced sideways and said curtly, 'No, Saskia.'

Confused, she thought at first she must have missed something else he had said. 'Sorry? I...'

'I didn't have an affair with Claudia,' he muttered, and then strode forward to join Jamie, who was admiring the clustered willow trees above the banks, their vivid greeny yellow knotted branches just budding into leaf.

Saskia drew a long, stunned breath. It was happening all the time—Domenico kept tapping into her thoughts, picking up her feelings. He never had while they were married. He had seemed blind to what was going on inside her then; even when she had tried to explain her feelings he hadn't understood them. Yet now he seemed to be recognising her emotions before she did. The change bewildered, confused her.

She became aware of the two bodyguards hovering behind her, obviously waiting for her to move, watching her like hawks.

Pulling herself together, Saskia hurried after Jamie and Domenico. It had stopped raining; the sky was still cloudy but there were patches of bright blue here and there, and a fitful sunshine kept shining through.

The elaborately wrought iron gates had been unlocked and stood open, but as soon as they had walked through them the gates were closed and locked again. Saskia glanced back to see the porter standing by the gates watching them, and through the ironwork she saw the two bodyguards standing on the bank. They were not coming inside; no doubt there were other men somewhere inside the grounds, watching them now, from a polite distance, but always on guard, always alert for trouble.

A shiver ran down her spine. She had hated living like this; she hated remembering now how it had felt.

Jamie was unaware of any of it; he was too eager to get into the gardens, flushed with excitement as he stared at a row of cherry trees foaming with white blossom which now stood between them and the house.

Through the trees you could see a green vista ending in that elegant white façade which they had glimpsed from the canal; the classical triangular pediment, perfectly proportioned windows, and the grace of the columned portico shimmered in the after-rain sunlight like a watery dream.

'Do you want to see the house or the gardens first?' asked Domenico, seeing them staring at it.

Jamie dithered, torn between the gardens, which were his obsession, and a feeling that he ought to look at the

Palladian house because that would be what most visitors would choose to see first.

'Well... if you think... that is...' He couldn't bring himself to make the decision, and asked politely, 'What would you like to show us first?'

Domenico gave him a dry look. 'I intended to offer you lunch, so we could leave the house until this afternoon.

Jamie's face relaxed, lighting up. 'That would be wonderful, thank you; I'm sure it's beautiful and... but we're here to advise you on the gardens, after all.'

They walked along a path skirting the cherry trees and Jamie paused to stare at the gardens in front of them: overgrown, untended, with here and there broken stone columns, or maimed statues, some with no heads, some with a hand or arm missing, bandaged with green moss or lichen the colour of mustard. They passed a wrecked gazebo with brambles and creeping bindweed growing through it, swags of ivy thickly clambering over walls, paths muddy and choked with weeds and grass, moss flowing down steps which led up towards the house. It was a gardener's nightmare, a ruin; yet spring was giving the place a beauty it wouldn't have in winter: among the weeds grew white narcissi, yellow tulips, purple hyacinths, and everywhere there were shrubs in flower, fruit trees in blossom.

'I told you it hadn't been touched for years,' Domenico shrugged.

Jamie laughed. 'You didn't exaggerate—but it wouldn't take long to clear most of the overgrowth and get back down to the original design.'

'That's what I decided. So I left this part of the garden alone while I was having the house modernised.'

'Well, as you probably know, you should never start working on an old garden for at least a year, anyway. You need to watch it through all four seasons to get some idea of what's already there.'

'Exactly. And my gardeners had enough to do laying down new lawns on the other side of the house, on a plot of land I was able to buy from the house next door, to give myself more space.'

Jamie peered at a bush he had just spotted. 'Is that a japonica?'

'I have no idea,' Domenico said drily. 'I'm not a gardener. That's why I need an expert to advise me on this English-style rose-garden I want; I thought it should be a sunken garden, with arbours, and pergolas. I've seen them in English country houses; they make nice places to sit in on summer days and they have atmosphere.'

'Oh, they do!' Jamie said with enthusiasm. 'Had you any colours in mind? Some people like a rose-garden in one colour—white, say, or yellow, or red. We laid out an all-white rose-garden for someone not long ago, didn't we, Saskia? It looked wonderful.'

'The roses didn't have much scent, though,' Saskia said honestly. 'If you go for colour you can't always have perfume too.'

'But if you want both we can find the right roses; it's simply a matter of knowing your roses,' Jamie said, frowning at her, afraid she might put Domenico off. 'And we'd be happy to send you our rose catalogue, with our recommendations for the plants which would suit you, so that you can browse through everything we have to offer, and make your own choices.'

'I have some rose books in my library; I have been doing some browsing already,' Domenico said with a faint smile. 'So, why don't I take your assistant to my library, and show her the roses that attract me, while you explore the garden and tell me if you have any views on the best way to re-establish the original design of the sixteenth century?'

Saskia opened her mouth to protest, her nerves jumping, but Jamie was too fast for her. Beaming, he said, 'Certainly. I'm free to just wander about, am I? I mean, it is safe to explore?' He looked over his shoulder nervously towards the gates through which they could still see the two bodyguards.

Domenico's mouth twisted. 'Perfectly safe, in these grounds—don't worry.' He put a hand into the pocket of his jacket and pulled out a small radio telephone, pulled up the aerial, tapped out a number, spoke into it rapidly in Italian.

Pushing the telephone back into his pocket, he said to Jamie, 'My head gardener is coming along to meet you; he speaks good English and he'll be happy to show you round.'

Jamie still looked faintly apprehensive. 'Have you told him we might be helping to design the rose-garden? Does he...I mean, will he...do you think he might resent foreigners muscling in on his territory?'

Domenico laughed. 'He worked in England on a big country estate for two years, getting experience; I don't think you need to worry. Get him to tell you all about the Duke; he loves talking about the noble family he worked for... Pietro was taken on by them specifically to look after a very old, and apparently enormous vine they had growing in a long glasshouse against the back wall of their great house. He's a specialist; they wanted him to improve the quality and quantity of the grapes they got from their vine.' He looked round as a man came hurrying through the trees. 'Ah, here he is!'

The new arrival was a man of about forty, tall, thin, wiry, with rough curls of black hair clustered on his head, olive, weatherbeaten skin, the skin of a man used to being out in the sun most of the day, and dark eyes like raisins, the skin around them wrinkled from being constantly screwed up against the sun.

Domenico said rapidly, 'Pietro Baldacci...this is Jamie Forster, who runs a garden centre in England...'

He did not introduce Saskia, nor did Pietro look at her or ask about her, but then he wouldn't. She stared at the ground, her face white. Pietro hadn't changed an inch. She should have guessed that Domenico would have him here to supervise the remodelling of these gardens: Domenico had a very high opinion of Pietro; he trusted him completely. How many other people from the Milan household had moved with Domenico to Venice? Her stomach clenched in shock and apprehension.

Pietro was being very discreet; presumably Domenico had warned him not to say anything to her.

Would they all be as politely blank, revealing nothing in their faces, in their manner towards her?

She dreaded meeting them again, knowing that they must be dying of curiosity, guessing at their disapproval, their hostility.

Pietro was an exception; he had been kind to her from the beginning, but then Pietro was a quiet, gentle man, a man used to his own company out in the open air, a man who rarely spoke, but was tolerant and kind-hearted.

She remembered his startled, incredulous face when she told him that she had worked as a gardener when she left school. Then he had smiled and told her with indulgence about the eccentric mother of the English duke he had once worked for, and how she, too, liked to garden in the afternoons.

Saskia hadn't tried to explain that that was different, that she was not an eccentric English lady, she had really worked at gardening, it had been how she earned her living, because she was poor, not rich, like the Duke's mother. She had chosen to work outdoors because she hated the thought of working in an office, and she had happened to see an advertisement in the local newspaper for a trainee to work in the local civic parks. She had applied, and been given the job simply by default because nobody more suitable had wanted the job. The head gardener in the parks department had been quite scandalised to be sent a girl, and had been convinced

that she would soon leave once she had realised how
hard the work could be, so he had begun the way he
meant to go on, teaching her the back-breaking jobs first.
Digging and forking compost into the soil, working on
the giant compost heaps they had hidden away behind
hedges in a corner of the park, learning tree surgery,
helping to lay paths and carry stone blocks here and
there. It had been a tough, exhausting job, but Saskia
had been good at it, and in the end even the head gardener had grudgingly had to admit she was, 'Quite a
useful little worker! And may make a gardener yet!'

After she married Domenico she had missed gardening; she had missed the satisfying exhaustion of
working out in the open air for hours, and had watched
Pietro enviously for months before she had finally
plucked up the courage to ask him if he would mind if
she did some gardening now and then.

He had been taken aback and couldn't hide his
amazement. But she was his employer's wife; if she
wanted to play at gardening Pietro was ready to indulge
her. All the same, at first he had kept a wary eye on her
activities, expecting her to do little but cut flowers or
wander about enjoying the sunshine.

Once he had seen to his barely concealed surprise how
much she knew, how thorough had been her grounding,
though, he had begun to trust her, and in time would
work alongside her, in the gardens in which he took such
pride, pruning and deadheading roses, taking cuttings,
layering rhododendrons, taking seed to be sowed later,
and even letting her pick flowers for the house, a task
he had always reserved for himself.

She had fled to the gardens in search of refuge, of
course. Pietro must have guessed that; no doubt that
was why he had been so kind to her, sensing how troubled
and uncertain she was, a very young girl out of her depth
in the grand house in which she was living. Some of the
servants working in the house had not been so kind or

so sympathetic; they had taken their cue from the family, looking down on her as an interloper without background, money or family. She hoped none of them had moved here with Domenico.

'We will begin in the Long Walk,' Pietro told Jamie at that moment. 'You are ready?'

'Yes, thank you.' But Jamie hesitated, giving Saskia a doubtful look. 'Will you be OK?' he murmured and she forced a smile.

'Yes, of course, fine.' She did not want Jamie being worried about her. She felt Pietro's eyes flick to her then away again quickly. What was he thinking? How much had Domenico told him? She liked Pietro; she didn't enjoy knowing that he must disapprove of her, be angry with her.

'See you later, then!' Jamie said, following Pietro into a tangle of shrubberies long grown out of all shape. Birds flew up on all sides, calling angrily. From the look of the garden few people had ever walked through it, let alone made any attempt to work on it. The birds were not used to human invasion.

Domenico looked down at her. 'We'll have to climb a lot of steps, I'm afraid, to get to the house, and they're overgrown with moss, and very slippery, so be careful, won't you?'

The cracked and broken steps rose up through encroaching shrubs, forsythia already thick with yellow buds of flowers, magnolias showing white chalice-like blooms on their crooked, twisted branches. Domenico kept a step behind her.

A large black and white bird flew out suddenly, from the thicket of shrubs, right into Saskia's face. She felt the brush of its feathers and fell backwards with a sharp cry. Domenico caught her with his body, deftly twisting sideways to impede her fall, his arms going round her as she crashed into him.

They rocked for a few seconds on the steps; Saskia thought they were both going to go tumbling down, but Domenico managed to stay upright.

'Are you OK?' he asked huskily.

Her heart was beating heavily, rapidly, against her breastbone; she couldn't breathe.

She nodded, deeply aware of him, his human warmth, his own heart beating, his quickened breathing, the power of his long, supple body.

Still holding her waist in one arm, he urged her up the final few steps to the wide, gravelled path running from one side of the garden to the other. The garden had been built on terraces, in fact, and at each level one of these wide paths ran horizontally, intersected by narrower paths of steps running vertically from the top to the bottom, but this structure only became clear as you moved through the garden; it could not be glimpsed from below because of the overgrowth sprawling all over the paths, hiding the design.

Now that they were safely on level ground Saskia tried to wriggle out of his grasp, her eyes lowered, her face flushed.

Silently, Domenico tightened his grip on her, and bent his head, his mouth hunting for hers.

'No!' she whispered, head averted.

His hand came up and caught her chin, tilted her head backwards, making her look up at him.

Saskia didn't want to; she was afraid of seeing his face, afraid of him seeing hers. She shut her eyes. She already knew how he was feeling; she did not need to read his mind. Her body was reading his body, perspiration had sprung out on her skin, her blood was beating wildly in her ears, deafening her.

'Look at me!' he muttered, shaking her.

Her eyes flew open, met his; she drew a sharp, savage breath at what she saw in his eyes, and then his mouth took possession of hers and she was lost.

Even when they were locked in bitter hostility they had always been able to forget everything else in bed, for a short while, their bodies melting in a desire so hot it consumed them both.

For a time Saskia had thought it would be enough. She had fooled herself into hoping that their marriage could work on that level alone, making it endurable for her, making it possible to bear the pain and bitterness of their life outside the bedroom. At last, though, she had been forced to see that desire was not love, passionate sex was not marriage; it was not enough; and so she had left him.

Now she was back in that old trap, imprisoned in passion, giving in to it helplessly, her mouth moving hotly against his, her hands restless, touching, exploring the hard male body pressing into her, deeply conscious of his hands and where they went, how they aroused the following blood in her veins as they stroked and caressed and discovered her.

When Domenico lifted his head at last she was as weak as a kitten, trembling, out of breath, her head swimming; she had to hang on to him to stay on her feet, her eyes still shut because she was afraid that if she opened them the world would be going round and round.

She felt him looking down at her and hid her face against his warm, rough sweater, felt the wool scratch her soft skin, was intensely aware of the sensation, of every sensation, as if her nerve-ends had been sensitised and quivered in shock at everything she touched or felt.

There was a long silence.

'Why?' Domenico burst out harshly, his hands closing over her arms, and her eyes flew open and she looked up at him in panic.

His face was dark with anger, his eyes were like hot coals, burning down into her.

'Why?' he asked again through his teeth, shaking her so that her head flew backwards and forwards. 'Why did you leave me? How could you do that to me? That note you left didn't explain, didn't tell me anything, just said you were going and not coming back and not to look for you. Not look for you! How could you think I wouldn't? Did you really believe I'd let you go like that? You must have known I'd go crazy, wondering where you were, what was happening to you...you must have known what you had done to me, vanishing like that. I don't think I slept for days; I couldn't work, or even think about business, I was distracted with worry over you, especially as I didn't know why you had gone. Why, Saskia? Why did you do it?'

At first she listened with regret, moved by the deep feeling in his voice, then a flare of rage lit her mind. She remembered the day she left, her own pain and fear and misery. He only seemed to see his own feelings, to be blind to hers. Had he ever tried looking at it from her point of view? No, of course he hadn't. He just blamed her; everything that had happened had been her fault; that was how Domenico saw it.

'Why did I leave?' she repeated thickly. 'Because I had to get away from you!'

He looked as if she had punched him in the stomach. White, his mouth opened, his breath drawn audibly.

He let go of her, his hands falling to his sides, screwed up as if to stop him doing something violent.

She involuntarily jumped back, afraid he was going to hit her. His eyes were black with raw emotion: explosive, volcanic.

'What?' he whispered at last. 'What are you saying, what do you mean?'

'I had to get away from you; I couldn't bear any more. How could I go on living with you knowing that you blamed me for...?'

She couldn't go on; tears were welling up in her eyes, and she was afraid they were going to spill out. Her throat was choked with silent sobs. She was trembling violently.

Domenico took a step towards her, his face tense and grim.

Saskia put out her hand, barring his way.

'N-no!' she stammered. 'Don't...don't touch me...' Angrily, she rubbed a hand across her wet eyes, swallowing, fighting to calm down.

When she felt she could, she huskily said, 'Don't deny it, Domenico. I know you blamed me, just as you blamed me when I had that fall and...and lost...had my accident. You shouted at me, said I'd been careless, I should never have been working in the garden.'

He was whiter than ever. 'That isn't true, Saskia, I didn't...I'm sure I didn't shout at you. OK, I was upset...'

'Angry! You were angry! Don't pretend I'm lying, or mistaken, because we both know it's true.'

He ran a hand through his hair, sighing. 'I suppose I was angry but not with you, only because you had taken the risk of working in the garden when you were pregnant, but I certainly did not shout at you.'

'You did; if you think you didn't it's because you're blanking it out, consciously or unconsciously. And as for me working in the garden...good heavens, I couldn't spend nine months lying on a couch, just because I was pregnant!'

'If you had, you would have carried the baby full-term, though!' he said curtly, and she winced.

'That isn't fair. How do you think most women manage? They carry on cleaning their houses, going to work, shopping, gardening, leading normal lives, and they have perfectly healthy babies.' She stopped, close to tears again, then fiercely added, 'I had an accident, Domenico! It wasn't my fault; it started to rain and I was hurrying indoors and I slipped and fell over—it could have happened in the street, while I was out shopping, or anywhere, doing anything. It was an accident, Domenico! But you blamed me for it!' Her voice shook. 'I'll never forget your face; you looked at me as if you hated me!'

'You can't have believed that,' he said in a low, husky voice, his face sombre. 'You knew I loved you! If I upset you, I'm sorry; believe me, Saskia, that was the last thing I wanted to do. But I'd been so happy about that baby; I wanted it so much...'

'Do you think I didn't?' Her blue eyes were almost black with pain.

'I know you did; I know how badly you felt about losing it, but I felt terrible, too, Saskia. When I first heard the news I almost went out of my mind. I rushed to the hospital to get to you.'

'Oh, yes,' she said, her face bitter. 'You came into that room and looked at me as if you hated me. I thought you were actually going to hit me; you stood by my bed shouting at me and the nurses came running in. They looked as terrified as I felt; they thought you were going to hit me, too.'

Even whiter, he bit out, 'I've never hit a woman in my life! I loved you; how can you accuse me of...?'

'You didn't see your face! You looked as if you were capable of anything! You frightened the life out of me.'

'I was still in shock! Saskia, it's you who's being unfair. I'd only just heard; I didn't know exactly what had happened, I didn't know how ill you were, I was worried and...oh, there were all these painful feelings swirling about inside me; I didn't know how to deal with what I felt, how I felt. Nobody teaches men how to cope with emotions, with pain and loss and fear...' He stopped, his throat moving convulsively as he swallowed. 'But you can't ever have thought I hated you. You always claim you can read my mind, so you must have known I loved you, even though I was so upset.'

Her eyes dark, she shook her head. 'It was because I could pick up what you were feeling that I know what was really going on inside you.'

He shifted impatiently, frowning. 'And what if you're wrong? What if you're not really picking up my feelings at all, only a part of them? I may have been angry...but that didn't mean I didn't love you, or wasn't worrying about you... When I'm worried, I get angry, don't you see?'

'Can't you express love any other way? Does it always have to come out as anger?'

He sighed, his mouth taut, running a hand across his eyes as though trying to erase some dark vision he could see. 'God knows. I've never thought about it before, but maybe it does. You know my family needs to protect itself twenty-four hours a day—that sort of constant vigilance means endless tension. I've lived with tension for so long, it's a habit, I suppose.'

She bit her lip, her face uncertain. 'Does that explain your father, too?'

Domenico's eyes sharpened, narrowed. 'Sooner or later you've got to tell me what he said to you the day you left, Saskia. I know something happened to make you run away.'

She wearily shrugged. 'Oh, what does it matter? From the beginning your father made it crystal-clear that he resented me and thought you'd made a big mistake in marrying me. He told me once that I only had one thing going for me—I was young and healthy, and could give you sons; and when I lost the baby he was even angrier than you were. I'd failed, at the one thing he thought I would be good for...' She caught the look Domenico gave her and burst out angrily, 'Oh, don't look at me as if I'm crazy—I didn't need to read his mind; he told me that. He said you'd only married because you wanted to start a family, and if I couldn't give you a healthy child soon you would get rid of me and try again with someone else.'

Domenico swore under his breath.

She started, flinching. Any sort of violence had that effect on her now. She was emotionally, mentally scarred by the past. She always would be.

'Saskia...' Domenico tried to put an arm round her but she stepped back nervously, shaking her head.

'Don't, please...'

He stood still, frowning. 'Saskia, I'm sorry for whatever my father said; you mustn't take too much notice of him.'

'I knew he was right, though. That day in the hospital... you were so angry...'

'Of course I wanted children,' he impatiently said. 'But more for my father than myself; he was desperate for grandsons, and he's so old, time's running out for him. I love my father, but I've always been a bit in awe of him; he was quite old himself, you know, when I was born, and he can be intimidating...'

'Yes,' she said with a bitter smile. 'He can!' She knew all about that. Giovanni had terrified her.

Domenico gave her a quick, frowning look. 'It was an obsession with him because my mother kept having daughters; it almost drove him mad when girl after girl arrived, and never a son, until at last I was born. Saskia, he's an old man with set ideas; it's too late to change him or his attitudes.'

'Attitudes you inherited from him!'

'No, Saskia! That isn't true. My father's mind is very different from mine—he was born in another world, before the First World War altered the map of Europe and destroyed many families like ours. Italy was another place then; my father grew up in a world of privilege and aristocratic values. He's obsessed with family. Ours is a very old family, Saskia, remember. The more the world has changed around him, the more he has clung to the old ways and old values. He places far too much importance on the idea of male heirs, to carry on our family. If my mother had had many sons instead of many daughters and only one son, my father might have come to terms with this new world we live in, but he's too old to change; you can't reason with him.'

Saskia thought of that last day, the old man's violence, her own fear, her sudden realisation that if she did not get away he'd kill her. Domenico didn't understand yet—his father had lost all contact with reason. He walked the borders of madness; his obsession with his family line had pushed him close to the edge.

'Where is he living now, still in Milan?' she asked.

Domenico shook his head. 'He's living just outside Padua.'

That surprised her. Surely Giovanni wasn't living alone? Perhaps he was living with one of his daughters? Giovanni had been living with Domenico when she married him; he had stayed on, a major cause of the strains on her marriage which had split them apart. Living with in-laws was never easy; it was impossible with a man as domineering and hard to please as Giovanni Alessandros.

'Have you sold the house in Milan?' she asked politely, wanting to keep their talk on a social level, to stop raw emotion erupting again.

'No, my sister Anna and her family are living there. Her husband is managing the Milan hotels; it's quite convenient for them.

Saskia smiled suddenly. 'How is Anna? She was always the nicest of your sisters—to me, I mean ... She's kind and she's funny. I used to enjoy going shopping with her; she made everything seem such fun. I really miss her.'

Domenico's face tightened. 'But not me, Saskia? You didn't miss me?'

She looked away, trembling, glancing up the narrow flight of steps which led at last to the gleaming white façade of the Palladian house. 'I thought you were going to show me round the house?' she hurriedly reminded him.

Domenico laughed shortly. 'Anything rather than talk about me? Very well, Saskia, come and see the house.' He put a hand through her arm and when she stiffened said with irony, 'We don't want you falling again, do we?'

She decided not to make an issue of it.

He gave her a mocking, sideways smile. 'Remember, I can read *your* mind now, Saskia!'

She ignored that, too, and he laughed.

As they climbed up the last flight of steps he talked about the house—when it had been built, how it had come into his family.

'You remember, Saskia, that Alessandros is a Greek name, although our family have lived in Italy for as far back as we can trace... they were obviously from one of the Greek settlements in Southern Italy, which have been there for two thousand years or more. This house was built for a Venetian family called Salvati, but during the nineteenth century one of my great-great grandfather's younger brothers married the only daughter of the man who owned this villa, and it was their grandson, my great-uncle, who died and left the place to me. He had two sons, both killed in the last war, leaving him without an heir, poor old man. He became very eccentric after the death of his wife, which is why the house was so neglected.'

As they reached the portico with its gleaming white columns a large Alsatian dog came shooting out from the open door and headed straight towards them.

Saskia stopped dead, freezing.

The Alsatian leapt for her, making frantic noises, and she dropped to her knees and held it, half in tears as it tried to lick her face, whining with excitement and joy.

'Suki! Oh, Suki!' She looked up at Domenico. 'Why didn't you tell me you had her here?'

'You didn't ask about her.'

She fondled Suki's ears, stroked her, got to her feet with the dog gambolling around her, still wild with the pleasure of seeing her again.

'It's amazing—even after all this time, she still remembers me!' she said unsteadily.

'Dogs never forget.' His tone was dry, sardonic; she heard the unspoken words and winced, but didn't reply. She was not going to tell him that she had not forgotten, either. He already knew too much about her feelings; she wasn't betraying anything else to him.

CHAPTER FIVE

IT TOOK an hour for Domenico to show Saskia round the house. As they came back down the massively beautiful staircase to the marble-floored entry hall Jamie walked through the open front door and stopped dead, mouth open as he took in his first glimpse of the house.

He whistled.

Saskia ruefully laughed. 'I know how you feel! Wait till you see the rest of it!'

Domenico watched them, his mouth reined tight.

Saskia had discovered as they went from room to room that he loved this house, and, although she was over-awed by all the marble and gilt and echoing, high ceilings, she had to say she also sensed a warmth here, not quite homeliness, but certainly a welcoming feeling which surprised her. She wasn't sure it would feel like that in winter, but now, in spring, with sunlight flooding the rooms and the scent of flowers on the air, you had to admit it was beautiful.

'You really live here?' Jamie asked Domenico with a comical expression. 'Isn't it like living in a museum?'

Saskia held her breath, waiting for Domenico to explode.

She saw his eyes glitter, felt the anger inside him. Domenico's instinctive hostility to Jamie hadn't shown yet. He had been pleasant enough in the hotel yesterday, and on the boat this morning, but his real feelings were very different and he no longer needed to hide them since he had achieved his real aim of getting Saskia to this house.

Realising he might have said the wrong thing, Jamie hurriedly added, 'Your garden, now, that's wonderful. I've been all over it. Did you know that you had some very rare species out there? I found a...'

His voice died away as he realised how Domenico was inspecting him, his cold eyes running from his dishevelled hair and grubby face down over his clothes to his muddy boots.

'You appear to have brought a lot of my garden in here with you,' Domenico drawled.

Jamie himself looked down at his clothes, liberally adorned with a dusting of yellow pollen, ivy, bits of grass, a trailing branch of bramble and a long stem of what in England was called Cleavers, a weed which attached itself to animals and people with tiny prickles, and had to be forcibly detached by hand.

'I am a mess, aren't I?' Jamie agreed amiably, grinning. 'It's a bit of a jungle out there, you know. I felt I ought to have a machete with me at times. The sooner you clear it, the better, but don't let any cowboys in there, will you? Because buried among all that undergrowth there are some very special plants and shrubs and it would be a tragedy if you lost them before an expert assessed which are still worth keeping and which are past their best. Even with those, you should take cuttings before you get rid of them. I didn't recognise a number of shrubs I saw, but I'm pretty sure they're rare and would be very interesting to other enthusiasts.'

'Thank you for the advice,' Domenico tersely retorted, making Jamie flush and look puzzled, and who could blame him? He had no idea why his host was looking at him as if he were a slug in his lettuce.

Saskia moved restlessly, frowning, and got a quick look from Domenico.

Before she could intervene, though, he said more politely, 'Before we have a drink and then lunch, I'm sure you want to wash and tidy up.' Domenico pressed a round brass circle set in the marble wall and almost at once a door opened at the end of the hall and a middle-aged man in a dark suit appeared.

For a second Saskia was tense, staring at him, but she had never seen him before in her life. He had not worked for Domenico in Milan.

'Mr Forster needs to wash and brush his clothes, Adriano.'

The man nodded, said to Jamie, 'If you would follow me, sir?'

Jamie gave Saskia a wordless glance, his eyes very expressive, full of disbelief, rueful laughter, then followed the servant, their footsteps echoing on the marble.

'How many of the servants did you bring with you from Milan?' she asked Domenico, who gave her a penetrating stare.

'None.'

Her eyes opened wider. 'None of them? But...hadn't they been with your family for years, some of them?'

'They still work for the family; they stayed on with Anna and her husband.'

'Oh, they didn't want to leave Milan?'

'I didn't want them,' Domenico said tersely.

Why hadn't he wanted to bring them here? Saskia wondered, watching him. Because in coming to this new home, in this new region of Italy, he was starting again, afresh? But there was something else she wanted to say to him.

'Did you have to look at Jamie as if he was an enemy, or talk to him like that? It wasn't fair. Jamie's such a nice man, Domenico; he's kind and good-hearted. He's been a very good friend to me.'

Domenico's eyes glittered. 'Maybe I don't like the idea of my wife having such close male friends!'

The biting tone made her stiffen.

'We went through all this yesterday, Domenico! Why won't you accept that Jamie's just a friend?'

'Even if I did think that that was all there was to it, I still wouldn't like it!'

Hot colour ran up her face. 'Do you know what century this is? Practically the twenty-first! Men and women do work together all the time; they even go on holiday together without it meaning a thing. The days when women were kept in a harem by their father or husband, away from other men, are long over, Domenico. I work for Jamie, nothing more; there has never been a word spoken between us that you couldn't have heard, he has never laid a finger on me, and I'm absolutely certain he'd be horrified if you accused him of being romantically interested in me.'

Her raised voice echoed in the high-ceilinged, marble-floored hall, and she broke off, biting her lip. Turning away, she walked into the gold and cream salon which led off the hall, and where, Domenico had told her earlier, they would be having drinks before lunch.

He followed close behind her and caught her arm, spun her round, so that their bodies almost touched, his eyes intense, possessive.

'No man with blood in his veins could look at you and not want you!'

Her skin burned with hot colour and she pulled away, shaking her head, the smooth bell of dark auburn hair swinging softly against her flushed cheeks.

'Stop talking like that!'

'Why should I? It's the truth.'

He came close again, she took another backward step, but she couldn't help a leap of awareness of him, of the casual, animal grace of his lithe body, the sensuality of mouth and skin, the hardness of bone, of powerful muscle, the flat angles of form, which were so alien to her own softer, rounder femininity, and yet attracted it so deeply.

'I know my own sex,' he whispered. 'You're beautiful, Saskia. Don't tell me Forster hasn't noticed that, because I wouldn't believe it, unless the man is officially blind.'

She couldn't help laughing at that. 'Look, I tell you he just doesn't fancy me; I'm not his type.'

'Is he yours?'

'No, Domenico!'

Their eyes met, held; she couldn't breathe, her mind taken over without warning by memories of making love to him, of lying naked in his bed, his dark head on her breast, his thigh moving restlessly against her, his hands tender, caressing, the weight of his body deeply satisfying, arousing a deeper need to absorb him, take him into herself.

'Saskia,' he whispered hoarsely, and with a pang of wild shock she stared into his eyes and knew that the images had come from his mind; he had sent them to her, like a radio station emitting signals through the receptive air. Domenico had discovered that he could not only read her mind but somehow feed his own thoughts into her.

'How did you do that?' she whispered back, as if afraid to admit aloud what had happened.

'I don't know. You're the expert, you tell me!'

He sounded genuinely baffled, half incredulous, almost angry. She frowned.

'But you knew you could?'

He shook his head. 'No, I knew I had, that's all; I knew when you started remembering too. It was weird, like hearing an echo—I just knew we were both sharing the same memory.'

She breathed unsteadily, looking away. He knew what she had thought, felt, wanted.

His face darkly flushed, he said thickly, 'Never mind all that telepathy stuff, it isn't important, but this is!' He took her face between his hands, his palms warm against her skin; she was taken by surprise, their mouths meeting a second later. The shock of desire was too sudden, too piercing, for her to fight it. Her blood sang in her ears, her mouth parted, hungrily kissed him back, an ache beginning deep inside her.

He gave a deep murmur of satisfaction and slid his arms round her, pulled her closer until their bodies merged, moving restlessly even closer. Her legs began to tremble, she put her arms round his neck and clung, her head falling back under the force of his kiss.

He lifted his mouth slightly a few moments later and looked down at her through half-closed lids, his skin hot, his eyes fierce.

'I knew it. You still feel the same. And so do I, darling. Come back to me, Saskia. We can start again here, in a new house, away from anything that could remind us of the past.'

For a second she was unbearably tempted; he was right, she loved him as much, almost more, because the pain she had suffered had deepened and strengthened her love. Worse, she wanted him more. Desire was beating deep inside her like a feverish pulse; she would have died to have him just once more, to feel the wild crescendo rise within her.

But two years ago she had been through hell. She could not risk it again.

'I can't!' she cried in anguish, and broke away from him. She got behind an elegant, cream brocade-covered chair, faced him defiantly as he took a step towards her. 'No! Stay away from me!'

He stopped, face taut, pale now. 'OK. But at least explain, Saskia. Don't I deserve an explanation? Why you left me? Why you won't come back?'

Her blue eyes were shadowed with pain and regret. 'You know why! You want children and I couldn't, never again...I couldn't bear it if it happened again.'

Watching her intently, his face shuttered and his mind now shuttered too so that she had no idea what he was thinking, he said quietly, 'There's no reason why you shouldn't have a perfectly healthy baby the second time.'

'The doctor told me I might always have a problem carrying a child full-term, you know that!' Tears burnt under her lids.

Domenico pushed the chair out of the way and put his arms round her, pushed her head down on to his shoulder.

'Don't, darling, don't.'

For a second she leaned on him, trembling, weeping, but she couldn't give in to that weakness. She had to be strong enough to bear it without him; she must not give in to the temptation of leaning on his strength.

She straightened, pushed him away, found a handkerchief in her pocket, wiped her eyes, blew her nose.

Domenico watched her, pushing his hands into his pockets, his face pale and tense.

'Saskia, that was one man's opinion—he could be wrong! Now that we know you have a problem we can work out ways of dealing with it. We'll get the best possible medical help and...'

'No!' she interrupted, her voice flat, weary. 'I'll never go through that again; I couldn't bear the hoping and then that awful moment when you know it's going wrong again...'

Domenico moved impatiently, restlessly. 'Saskia, everything is a risk. Life is built on taking risks. Even crossing a road can be a risk; you could be hit by a car any time.'

'Your family would be relieved if I were!'

The bitter little joke made him stiffen, look at her with a deeper frown.

'They weren't very friendly to you, were they? I'm sorry, Saskia. If I'd known...if you had said something...but I had no idea what was going on, how badly they were treating you; they didn't act like that when I

was around. It was only after you had left that Anna
told me what you had had to put up with from them.'

Her mouth relaxed a little; she gave a long sigh, half
smiling. 'Anna was always kind to me; she was the only
one who was,' she said again. Anna looked like
Domenico; she was the closest to him in age, too. Dark-
haired, olive-skinned, full-figured, she had a warm,
happy personality; she laughed a great deal, talked
quickly, was full of fun, adored by her three children
and by her clever, busy husband.

Anna's own life was crowded; she had a home to run,
she worked hard for a children's charity, threw dinner
parties, was always going to the theatre or the opera,
yet she had made room in her hectic whirl for this new,
much younger and very nervous and uncertain sister-in-
law who was cold-shouldered by everyone else in the
family. Anna had done her best to see that Saskia felt,
in spite of that, that she belonged in the Alessandros
clan.

'She was fond of you. When you vanished without a
word Anna was really upset; I can't remember ever seeing
Anna cry like that before.' Domenico's face was sombre.

Saskia bit her lip, touched and guilty. 'She really cried?
Oh, that's so... I should have written to her, explained,
but I didn't think about Anna; I ought to have done,
she had been so kind to me, but... I just had to get
away, at once; there was no time to think about anything
else.'

He stared at her intently; she felt him trying to read
her mind. 'Because of something my father said? I know
something happened that day, Saskia. When he heard
you had left for good, my father was so shocked, he had
a stroke.'

She drew a startled breath, blue eyes opening wide,
dark and incredulous. 'A stroke? Was it serious?'

Domenico's face was grim. 'For a few days we thought
he was going to die, but then he slowly began to recover.

But he has never been the same since—he can talk and even walk a little now, but it aged him; his hair went quite white and the stroke left his face faintly lop-sided so that he's scarcely recognisable as the same man.'

'I'm very sorry, Domenico,' she whispered. 'Your father was always so full of energy, it's hard to imagine him being ill.'

'His energy has almost gone now; in fact, he's a different man. It's as if a spring broke inside him the day you left.'

She flinched. 'I'm sorry,' she said again, helplessly, 'I know how much your father means to you.'

'I love my father,' Domenico agreed in a level voice. 'I love my sisters, too. Family is the most important thing in life—what else matters so much? But my family includes you, Saskia; you are part of my family now and forever, and the most important part, for me, don't you know that? You're my wife.' His eyes were grave, fixed, very intent. 'You know we're Catholics and I will never divorce you.'

She bent her head, regret aching inside her. 'Surely you could get an annulment?'

'Don't be ridiculous,' he snapped. 'That would only apply if we had never slept together, Saskia. There are no grounds for annulment and I would never consider asking for one, anyway. You will always be my wife, whether you live with me or not. My sisters should have remembered that.'

'Would it have made any difference? They were furious because you'd married a little nobody without either money or family connections. I think they had plans for you...'

He grimaced. 'They've always tried to interfere in my life—every so often they've produced some suitable girl, but I wasn't interested in any of them; my sisters know that perfectly well.'

'That didn't stop your sisters from deciding that I was a gold-digger who had managed to trap you into marrying me. Apart from Anna, your sisters hated me on sight. I had nothing in common with any of them. I didn't know anyone they knew, I had no background, or friends, I had never gone skiing in Gstaadt or watched polo at Windsor, or stayed on Long Island with wealthy American families. I came from another world altogether; I was from another class; the sort of person who waited on them, cooked their meals, did their garden. After all, they knew I'd worked for my living. I was an embarrassment to them.'

He looked even angrier. 'Is that what they told you?'

'They didn't need to say anything—their attitudes spoke louder than words.'

He brooded on her, his eyes dark, his mouth tense.

'Why on earth didn't you tell me what you were having to put up with? I'd have had it out with them. Anna says Maria Teresa was the worst—which doesn't surprise me—she's a silly, arrogant bitch, and she was always the ring-leader in whatever the others got up to! Carla and Oriana never had an idea of their own in their lives; they just followed Maria Teresa and copied everything she did.'

It was true. The two younger sisters were just echoes of their domineering older sister; only Anna, the youngest of all of them, except Domenico himself, had been free of Maria Teresa's bullying, overbearing authority, because there was such a big gap in time between her and her older sisters. She had grown up close to Domenico instead.

'They're still your sisters,' Saskia said quietly. 'And, as you just said, family comes first with you. They made my life impossible enough, but your father...' She broke off and felt his eyes questioning, probing, his brows black above them, anger in his face, in the air between them.

'Tell me, Saskia. Sooner or later you're going to have to tell me...what did my father say that day to make you run away? It must have been serious for him to have had a stroke later. So don't pretend it wasn't important; it's obvious it was.'

She moved restlessly, too upset to say anything, and Suki, lying at her side, lifted her sleek head, ears pricking, and looked at her, aware at once of her mistress's distress, growling softly, anxiously in her throat, ready to spring to Saskia's defence, if it were needed.

At that instant footsteps rang on the marble floor of the hall and Jamie came through the door into the gold and cream salon.

Saskia started in surprise; she had been so absorbed in Domenico that she had actually forgotten that Jamie was even in the house.

Domenico scowled. He had forgotten, too, and was infuriated by the interruption, especially at that moment.

Suki put two and two together. Her mistress was unhappy, her master was angry, and here was a strange man in their home, a man she sensed neither of them was pleased to see. She didn't wait to think it over, or wait for orders. She launched herself like a rocket at Jamie, snarling ferociously.

Jamie gave a gulp of horror and backed towards the door again, picking up the nearest brocade-covered, gilt-legged chair, using it to keep Suki away, like a lion-tamer, jabbing the legs at her as she tried to get at him.

'Leave him alone...down, Suki!' Saskia said, horrified, her nerves jangling.

Domenico snapped out an order, his tone sharper, hard with authority. 'Sit!'

The dog reluctantly sat, still growling in her throat, watching Jamie relentlessly, her tongue lolling out of her open jaws.

Domenico patted her head. 'Good girl.'

'Good girl?' repeated Jamie, pale and highly indignant. 'She nearly had my arm off!'

'She was defending us,' Domenico coolly told him. 'That's her job; she's a guard dog and you are a stranger; she didn't know why you were here, and decided she didn't like the look of you.' His tone implied that Suki had excellent taste.

'Well, I certainly don't like the look of her!' Jamie was shaken by what had happened; he was still gripping the chair in front of him, the legs pointing forward. 'I shan't feel safe while she's around; she's watching me in a very beady-eyed way, as if she's planning what part of me to go for the minute you give her the go-ahead. Could you put her somewhere else while we're here?'

As if understanding what he was saying, Suki wriggled backwards on her stomach, and put her head on Saskia's foot.

Saskia couldn't help smiling.

Domenico said softly, 'You see the problem? We'd have a problem persuading her to go anywhere. She won't let Saskia out of her sight again, if she can help it.'

Jamie gave him a puzzled look. 'Oh? Taken a fancy to Saskia, has she?'

'She's Saskia's dog.'

Saskia drew breath sharply, turned white.

Jamie looked at her, then back at Domenico again, frowning, trying to make sense of what was being said.

'You mean you've given her to Saskia?' He seemed lost for words for a second, dismay in his eyes, then he stammered, 'Well... that's very generous, very kind, of you... but... really, I mean, we won't be able to take her back to England, you know... it would be... quite impossible, you see...'

When he had stumbled into silence Domenico drawled, 'I haven't given her to Saskia, she already belonged to her. She was a present to Saskia when she was a puppy.'

Jamie's mouth opened, shut. He stared at Domenico, lowered the chair he was still holding, turned to stare at Saskia. 'What are you talking about? I don't understand... Saskia, what does he mean? How can the dog have belonged to you since she was a puppy? You never said you had a dog, and what is it doing here, anyway, if it is yours?'

Saskia was dumb; she couldn't get a word out.

Domenico did not have the same problem.

'She's my wife,' he said in the same calm voice.

Jamie looked as if he had been hit by lightning. 'She's your wife,' he repeated, as if trying to interpret words in a foreign language. 'She's your... what on earth are you talking about? What's going on here? Saskia?' He took two steps towards her. 'Saskia, what is this all about?'

Suki sat up and growled a threat, ready to spring again. Jamie stopped dead.

'Sit!' Domenico snapped again.

The dog sat, but was poised, waiting for any more orders, watching Jamie with bright, intent eyes.

'It's biding its time; it will have my throat out any minute!' protested Jamie.

'Down, Suki!' Domenico's voice cracked like a whip.

The dog lay down, with a gusty sigh, head on Saskia's foot again, tethering her to the spot as if afraid that otherwise she might vanish once more.

Domenico walked over, picked up a deep-cushioned chair, put it behind Saskia. 'And you'd better sit down, too, before you fall down.'

Like the dog, Saskia obeyed. He was right; her legs were trembling, almost buckling under her, she felt sick and faint. Domenico gave her a quick, searching look, frowned, walked across the room to a table loaded with bottles and glasses, slices of lemon and orange. 'I think we could all do with a drink before lunch. Forster, what would you like? I can offer you a wide enough choice... sherry, vermouth, gin and tonic, whisky?'

'Sherry, thanks.' Jamie was still staring at Saskia, his brows knit in abstraction.

Domenico shot him a glance. 'Sit down yourself, but if you're wise you'll keep well away from the dog.'

'Why do you have it around the house if it's that dangerous?' Jamie reproached.

'I keep it because it's dangerous,' Domenico drily told him. 'But it is no threat to me, or to Saskia, or anyone it knows. They're pack dogs; they guard their own, but attack strangers.'

'Including visitors, apparently,' Jamie muttered, going warily and slowly, keeping an eye on Suki, over to one of the cream brocade-covered sofas. He sat down at the end of it furthest from the dog.

Silence fell; the room was full of brooding—the dog brooded on Jamie, who was staring at Saskia, and she was staring out of the window, at the bright spring sunlight, her mind full of resentment. Domenico had had no business to tell Jamie like that, forcing the issue, knowing that she had not wanted to say anything yet. It was typical of him. He was so used to giving orders and having people jump to obey him, he couldn't brook any argument; he was too impatient, too sure he was always right.

He brought her a glass, pushed it into her hand, sat down next to her, on another chair, the two of them side by side, facing Jamie at the other end of the room.

Domenico leaned over and curled his fingers round her glass, tilted it to her lips, insisted, 'Drink some, Saskia!'

She gave him a cross look, but took a reluctant sip, coughed as the rich liquid ran down her throat, almost at once felt slightly warmer, her nerves less tense.

Jamie drank some of his sherry. 'So, are you going to explain, Saskia?' he asked wryly, and she saw that he was calmer now, he wasn't so angry any more.

'I'll explain,' Domenico told him coolly.

'I want to hear it from Saskia!'

They both looked at her. Her blue eyes were dark and unhappy. In a low voice, she said, 'I meant to tell you soon, Jamie, but... I hate talking about the past. I am his wife, but I left him two years ago, and went back to England, started using my maiden name again, got the job with you. I'm sorry I lied, if only by omission, not telling you that I was married; I was afraid Domenico would find me; I didn't want anyone to know I had ever been married.'

Jamie gave Domenico a scowl, then looked back at her. 'Is he threatening you, Saskia? If you're frightened of him, you don't need to be, not with me around!'

'Don't push your luck, my friend!' snarled Domenico, getting to his feet.

Suki sat up, too, her fangs bared, growling in her throat.

'I'm not scared of you, or your dog,' Jamie said belligerently, standing up to face them both.

'Stop it, both of you!' Saskia broke out, her voice shaking. 'Jamie, you don't understand the situation, and I don't want to talk about it, but he isn't threatening me, it's nothing like that... Please, don't get involved, leave it alone.'

There was a silence; Jamie stared at her fixedly, frowning and uncertain. Somewhere a telephone began to ring, stopped. A moment later a phone rang in the room and Domenico made a harsh, impatient noise, went over to pick it up.

'I thought I told you I didn't want to be disturbed,' he said in Italian. Then, 'What? Oh...' There was a moment's silence; he glanced over his shoulder at Saskia, his brows together. Then he said into the phone, 'Very well, give me time to get there, then put him through in the study.'

He replaced the phone, turned, said politely, 'Excuse me for a moment,' and left the room.

As soon as he had gone, Jamie sat down as if his legs had given way under him. Saskia put her hand on Suki's head, pushing the dog down too. Suki collapsed with another of her noisy sighs, her head going back on to Saskia's foot.

Jamie stared at her for a long moment, then broke out, 'I can't believe you didn't tell me! All this time! I've known you two years and you never breathed a word about being married, let alone married to someone like him!'

'I couldn't bear to talk about it; the wounds were still too raw.'

He thought that over, frowning. 'Can you bear to talk about it now?'

'No.'

Jamie grimaced. 'Oh, well, OK. But I can't get over the fact that you never breathed a word yesterday... when you first walked into that room and saw me with me... it must have been the biggest shock of your life, but I never picked up the slightest hint! Mind you, I did think you were in an odd mood, very quiet; I thought you must be shy... and all the time... honestly, Saskia, I can't get over it! Did he know you were in Venice, is that it? Did you let him know you were coming?'

She shook her head. 'I'd no idea he would be here. I thought he still lived in Milan. It was a terrible shock when I saw him.'

Jamie gazed, wide-eyed, shaking his head. 'It must have been. But... hang on! It can't have been a coincidence that he got into conversation with me... that would be too weird!'

'He saw us at the theatre the night before last,' she admitted.

Jamie took that in, laughed shortly. 'Which was why you suddenly developed toothache? You saw him, too? And insisted on leaving, rushing back to the hotel. No wonder you seemed feverish! I'm surprised you didn't get the next plane home.'

Wearily she said, 'I thought of it, but it was too late. He would have been able to get my address from the tour people; he'd have followed me if I had gone.'

Jamie inhaled sharply. 'You mean ... he hasn't had your address? He hasn't known where you were, all this time?'

She nodded.

Jamie whistled. 'You must be scared stiff of him to hide like that. What happens now? Did I bring you into a trap? My God, Saskia, you should have told me! I'd never have let this happen if you had!'

She gave him a wan smile. 'I'm not frightened of him, Jamie; I told you, it isn't like that. Domenico wouldn't hurt me. Once he had seen me, meeting him again was inevitable, and I suppose it was time we talked. But you mustn't think this is anything to do with you. It isn't.'

They both heard Domenico's quick, firm footsteps crossing the marble hall, the door opened and he walked rapidly into the room, looked at once at Saskia, his eyes compelling.

'That was my father on the phone. I told him I'd found you, and he asked me to beg you to come and see him, let him tell you he is sorry for everything he did to hurt you. He wants to make his peace with you before he dies, Saskia.'

CHAPTER SIX

SASKIA'S first reaction was to shake her head in panic, saying, 'No, I couldn't! Don't ask me to... I couldn't face him...'

Domenico's eyes were sombre, watchful; he didn't say anything for a moment, but Jamie looked shocked.

'Saskia! I can't believe it's you talking! If his father is dying, surely... I mean, good heavens, Saskia, that alters everything, doesn't it?' He stopped, gave Domenico an embarrassed look, his ears turning red. 'Sorry, none of my business, of course; I shouldn't interfere in family matters. It's just that I thought I knew Saskia, and today she's giving me surprise after surprise. I'd have sworn she was the last woman in the world to refuse to forgive a dying man.'

'I don't think she will, when she has thought it over,' Domenico said flatly, his eyes still fixed on her.

She gave a quivering sigh. She knew she would have to go, even though every nerve in her body was prickling with fear at the idea of facing Giovanni Alessandros again. Her last image of him had been so violent, so filled with hatred; it had haunted her day and night for months afterwards and still made her shiver when she remembered it.

Desperately, she protested, 'But we only have one more day in Venice; we'll be leaving Venice the day after tomorrow! There really isn't time for me to go to Padua and back.'

'We could fly there this afternoon, by helicopter,' shrugged Domenico. 'It wouldn't take long. You could be back in time for dinner, with luck.'

She wasn't going to get out of it; he was not going to let her. He was determined to make her see his father, and Jamie was looking at her with such bewilderment and dismay. He didn't understand. Why should he, when he didn't know what had happened between her and Domenico's father? She was trapped, helpless.

'You'll go there with me?' Her voice was heavy with resignation.

'I'll be there,' Domenico promised, his eyes grim. He despised her for making all this fuss about seeing his dying father, she thought, until he added, 'I won't leave you alone with him, I promise,' and with a leap of the heart she realised he wasn't angry with her, after all. How much did Domenico know?

She bit her lip. 'When will we leave?'

'We'll have lunch first. The helicopter isn't here; I'll have to get in touch with the pilot, get him to fly here to pick us up. We should be able to leave by three o'clock. You won't be with my father very long; he tires easily and it will be a strain for him to see you at all, but he won't rest until he does. Afterwards, I'll fly you back.' He glanced at his watch. 'I'll ring for lunch to be served at once. The first course is cold so it will be ready.'

Jamie looked faintly relieved, no doubt having begun to wonder if he was going to get lunch at all. After a morning in the open air he was probably starving.

As Domenico spoke to the servant, Adriano, Jamie leaned over to say apologetically to her, 'Saskia, I'm sorry; I'd no business criticising you. I expect you're embarrassed about seeing his father again, after your marriage break-up, but you know you're doing the right thing. You couldn't have refused a dying man.'

She looked at him wryly, managed a smile, nodded. Jamie was a very conventional man; he would never have hesitated, in her place, to make peace with the old man, but then Jamie didn't have complicated reactions to life, nor had he ever had to cope with anything more painful than putting a garden fork through his foot in an absent-minded moment. As far as she knew, Jamie had never been in love yet, nor did he have any problems with family or friends. Jamie was a cheerful, sunny soul doing a job he loved, leading a life he enjoyed. How could he understand the darkness which could invade a life without warning? He might understand if she explained everything, but she couldn't talk about so much of what had happened to her during her marriage.

Domenico was making his phone call to the pilot; Saskia half listened, was half lost in thought about his father, the ordeal in front of her.

Putting down the phone, Domenico turned to them again. 'That's all arranged; by the time we've had lunch the helicopter should be here. Adriano is serving the first course now—shall we start eating at once?'

They ate in a spacious dining-room with marble floors and walls painted with what Domenico told them was a Renaissance fresco of Roman banqueting: guests lying on couches around a table piled with amazingly lifelike fruit, a dancer undulating in fluttering gauze, a man playing a stringed instrument. The painting was confident, the colours soft, a little faded; it had been cleaned and restored by experts, Domenico said, since he inherited the house.

'I wonder if it was comfortable, eating like that?' Jamie thought aloud.

'Very uncomfortable, I'd have thought.' Domenico shrugged. 'I wouldn't be surprised if they all had indigestion.'

Their first course was a salad of mussels, prawns and tiny, boneless fish. *'Di frutti di mare,'* Domenico told Jamie when he asked the name of the dish.

'Fruit of the sea? It looks delicious fruit, too.' Jamie said, putting a pink prawn into his mouth.

'Oh, you know some Italian? *Buon appetito!'*

'*Grazie*,' said Jamie, adding quickly, 'I only know a few words!'

Domenico leaned over to fill Saskia's glass. 'This is Soave, a dry white local wine which goes well with fish,' he told her. 'Try it.'

She sipped a little, nodding.

'Good?' Domenico asked, looking into her eyes.

'Good,' she agreed, her mouth dry in spite of the wine. Every time she met his eyes she felt a leap of shock, of incredulous pleasure; she still couldn't believe she was in the same room, that he was close enough to touch.

'Look at that Cedar of Lebanon,' Jamie said in a rapt voice, gazing out of the window at an ancient cedar towering in the distance, enormous, dark green layers of dense foliage spreading horizontally from a vast bole. It dwarfed all the other trees around it—the laurels and Italian cypress, olive trees with silvery, fluttering leaves, a fig tree, a slip of a cherry already foaming with white blossom. 'Have you had it date-tested?' he asked Domenico.

'Date-tested?' Domenico's eyebrows rose. 'Why would I do that?'

'That cedar looks very old to me; look at the size of it, it's enormous—it might even be as old as this house. I'd have it checked if I were you. It's a simple process, almost infallible, and it would be fascinating to find out if it was planted when the house was built, or was even there first!'

'Yes, you're right, it would be!' Domenico said, staring at the tree as if he had never noticed it before. He had probably taken it for granted without questioning its age. 'I must find an expert to do it for me.'

Their fish was followed by lamb cutlets, coated in breadcrumbs and fried, served with a rich sauce which Jamie adored. Jamie had a good appetite because he worked hard every day in the open air. At home, he ate very simply but he had become engrossed in Italian cuisine since they arrived here and he discovered that Italian cooking did not begin and end with pasta, as he had always imagined.

'What's in this?' he asked Adriano, who was serving the meal with the help of a silent, olive-skinned young girl in a little black dress.

'This, sir?' Pleased with this interest, he explained, 'This is a white sauce, thickened with egg yolks, then flavoured with chopped truffles and little slivers of ham, and the lamb is served with young artichoke hearts, thin strips of spring cabbage cooked with ham and onion, and new potatoes.'

'I thought those pink strips in the sauce were ham! And the black bits are truffle? Well, it's gorgeous, I love it,' Jamie said and Adriano smiled, pouring red wine for them.

'I will tell my wife you enjoyed it, sir.'

'She cooked it? She's a treasure; tell her I envy you.' Adriano smiled again. 'I will, sir.'

'And what's this?' asked Jamie, trying to see the label on the bottle of wine.

'Bardolino, sir.'

'Local dry red,' Domenico expanded. 'Very good with lamb, I think, especially cooked like this.'

When Adriano and the girl had left them, Domenico asked Jamie, 'Did my gardener show you where we plan to have the sunken rose-garden?'

'Yes—I think it would be a good site, but you would have to have some remedial work on that soil before you plant any roses; your gardener seemed to have some very good ideas about that, though.' He paused, his face flushed and uncertain. 'You are going ahead with that project, then? It wasn't just something you dreamed up to get Saskia here?'

'No, it was not.' Domenico's face was cold, hostile.

Jamie looked nervously at him. 'Sorry if I offended you, but I just thought...'

'Are you surprised if he jumped to that conclusion?' Saskia intervened sharply, and Domenico shrugged at her.

'OK, maybe not, but I do have every intention of making a rose-garden. The actual construction work would be done by a local firm, but if your firm want to design it, and supply the English roses, Forster, then the contract is yours. You would be working with my own head gardener, who would be in charge here, and would make sure that your design was carried out by the local contractor. You wouldn't need to return here, unless you choose to come back to see the finished garden. My people would keep in touch with you by letter, or phone, or do you have a fax machine?'

'Yes, I do, and we'd be delighted to design the garden for you—and supply the roses.' Jamie was flushed with excitement. He looked at Saskia, then frowned. 'Oh. I hadn't thought...are you...?' He stopped, looked at Domenico nervously, hesitated, then asked her, 'Are you coming back to England, Saskia?'

Domenico sat very still, watching her.

'Yes,' she said, not meeting his eyes but feeling the threat in them like a wind from the north, icy and lethal.

Let him glare. He wasn't frightening her back to him. Nothing had changed, after all. His father might say he wished to make his peace with her, but she knew that the underlying hostility of the Alessandros family towards her would not have changed. She would always be the outsider, the unwanted intruder in their lives, the enemy.

Domenico might be angry with his sisters for treating her badly, but they were still his sisters, his father was still his father, and family came first with him, with all of them. It always would. She knew him.

Domenico had moved away from them, it was true; they would no longer be living so close, as they had when he lived in Milan and they were all near-by, always visiting him, phoning, inviting him to their homes.

She wouldn't have to put up with the scarcely veiled contempt and arrogance of old family friends, either—all those aristocratic old ladies and retired military men who had been the friends of Giovanni, who felt Domenico had married beneath him and were outraged at being asked to be polite to someone they viewed as a little nobody from nowhere, and foreign into the bargain!

But how could she ask him to cut himself off from his family and his oldest friends forever? Nobody had the right to demand that of a man in the name of love.

And that wasn't even the only barrier to their happiness. She would never again risk trying to have a baby. Even now, after two years, she still hadn't got over the agony of losing her baby, of going through what felt like childbirth without the happiness and comfort of a child at the end of it. It had been a painful miscarriage, she had suffered badly, but the worst moment had come when the gynaecologist who saw her in hospital told her that she would always have a problem carrying a child full-term. She had been stricken.

She couldn't ask Domenico to accept a childless marriage. She knew how badly he wanted children, sons; he might claim it was only his father who wanted heirs for the Alessandros name and fortune, but that wasn't true. Domenico had wanted them, too. She was sure he still did.

Surely her inability to give him children must be grounds for an annulment?

She felt Domenico trying to read her mind, felt the tension in his body. Once he accepted that she was never coming back surely he would try to have his marriage annulled so that he could marry again and get himself sons?

Jealousy gnawed inside her like a caged rat as her mind fed her pictures of Domenico with another woman;

marrying again, making love, someone else in his arms, some faceless woman entwined with him, their naked bodies moving on white sheets.

She pushed the images away, her hands clenched on her lap, out of sight of the two men, her nails digging into her palms, trying to drive out one pain with another.

Domenico went on watching her. She felt him trying to penetrate her mind again, and kept her eyes down, fighting to ignore him.

Adriano served their dessert, green figs or home-made water ice flavoured with peach or strawberries. Jamie contemplated them both indecisively.

'Have both,' suggested Domenico.

Jamie laughed. 'I'm being greedy, aren't I?'

'They're both very light.'

Saskia had lost all appetite but with Domenico watching her she forced herself to pretend to eat water ice, moving it around the fluted-glass dish while it melted back into liquid.

Adriano took it away when he cleared the table; he served her espresso coffee, black and strong.

'Adriano will take you back to Venice, Forster, immediately after lunch,' Domenico told Jamie over their coffee.

'Thanks,' Jamie said, giving him a hesitant look. 'Saskia will be back for dinner, definitely?'

'With any luck.' The short tone was not encouraging, but Jamie persisted.

'Only the tour organiser is bound to ask where she is and when we can expect her back; you know how bureaucratic these trips can be. The poor man has to account for all of us all the time.'

'You aren't responsible for Saskia, and neither is he. I'm taking her to Padua and I hope to get back here before dinner tonight. That's all you need to tell him.'

Jamie opened his mouth, met Domenico's steely eyes and closed his mouth again.

When Adriano appeared to escort him back to the canal Jamie gave Saskia a hug and whispered, 'Are you sure you'll be OK?'

Now that he was going she felt a surge of panic and almost begged him not to leave her alone with Domenico.

'Hurry up, the boat is waiting,' Domenico said sharply.

Jamie still hesitated. Saskia forced a reassuring smile, nodding. 'I'll be fine.' She didn't want Jamie to feel guilty about leaving her here. He would get nowhere if he tried to confront Domenico, for one thing; she didn't want Jamie to end up being hurled into the canal or have a black eye to show for his trip to the Brenta. Anyway, he was right—she had no option but to see Giovanni Alessandros and listen to whatever he had to say to her, however scared she was of meeting the old man again.

She stood under the portico in the afternoon sunlight watching Jamie walk down the terraces, between the wildly overgrown shrubs and trees, his figure diminishing all the time as he neared the iron gates through which the bodyguards could be seen waiting, their polite threat visible even at this distance.

Jamie paused, looked back; she could pick up his apprehension at the prospect of being alone with Adriano and the bodyguards on the boat back to Venice, but he waved and grimaced cheerfully.

She waved back, sighing. Poor Jamie.

'Sorry he's going without you?' Domenico asked curtly.

She was angry with him for putting it like that. 'I'm not looking forward to seeing your father again, if that is what you mean! I'm very sorry he is so ill, I don't wish him any harm, but he always frightened me, and I can't believe he has changed.'

'He has, Saskia,' Domenico said in a heavy voice. 'He hasn't long to live; it might be days, or weeks, it might even be a few months, but no longer than that, they tell me. It's a miracle he has hung on this long. I think he was waiting to see you again, tell you he was sorry for whatever he did to hurt you.'

His eyes were so watchful, his mind a net, trying to catch her thoughts.

'I thought the helicopter would be here by now?' She turned away, evading him.

The house echoed behind them; a lovely shell, full of the sound of the past, yet empty. But it wasn't empty, was it? You couldn't see or hear them, but somewhere there must be other people in the house.

'How many servants have you got here?' she asked him, wandering back into the cream and gold salon.

'Adriano and his wife, and some local girls who come in to do housework every day.'

He was right behind her. Her nerves were jumping again. So they were almost alone here; just Adriano's wife, in the kitchen, out of earshot.

'I'm surprised you didn't bring any of the servants from Milan; some of them had worked for your family all their lives, hadn't they?'

'Maybe that was part of the problem,' he said curtly. 'Maybe they thought they were family, and took their attitudes from my father and my sisters. Once Anna told me how they had been treating you I made up my mind that when I found you again and brought you home you would never have to put up with any of them again. I couldn't sack them, that wouldn't have been fair, but I found them all jobs with one or other of the family. The only one I kept with me was Pietro, because I knew you were fond of him, and he had been kind to you.'

'Pietro was wonderful to me. He was the only one I felt I could meet on an equal footing.'

Domenico drew a harsh breath. 'My God, why didn't you tell me, Saskia? Why go through all that on your own, locking it all inside yourself? If I had had the faintest inkling...!'

He tried to put his arms around her and she jumped away, swallowing convulsively.

'How do you run the business from here?' Her voice came out high and quivering.

There was a silence, then he said flatly, 'I have an office in the house; I didn't show it to you, but it has the latest office technology.'

He was close to her again. He pushed a tendril of dark auburn hair back from her flushed cheek and the brush of his hand against her skin made her tremble.

'I have two secretaries who come in most weekdays,' he said. 'They deal with mail and faxes, take phone calls. I can do a lot by phone.' His long index finger slid lightly down her spine.

She shivered, the little hairs on the back of her neck prickling. She took another step.

His voice went on calmly, 'Other days I go by helicopter to the airport, take a plane to have a board meeting in Milan, or visit one of our hotels somewhere else in Italy.' He was behind her again; she could feel his warm breath on her neck, he was so close. A tremor of passion shook her. 'We're thinking of branching out into Europe soon,' his voice softly said. 'All the big international hotel chains are on the move, biting into new territory, new countries. The hotel business is becoming European rather than national. My advisers tell me we must expand too, or find ourselves being pushed out of the market.'

She tried to move away again but he caught hold of her shoulders, pulled her back until their bodies were so close, a sheet of paper couldn't have been slid between them. He bent his head; his mouth moved against her throat.

'I dream about you, you know, night after night.'

She shut her eyes. She had dreamt about him night after night too. Had they dreamt the same dreams?

'Do you know what I dream?'

'No,' she lied. She knew. He was thinking about it now; she was shaking as the images flashed to her. She wished she could shut her mind to them, block them out, stop him projecting his thoughts to her, but she was weaker than he was; Domenico was beating down every barrier she put up against him.

'Saskia,' he whispered, and his mouth moved upwards slowly, kissing every inch of skin on its way to her mouth.

The pleasure overwhelmed her. Tactile, sensual, warm; his mouth on her skin, like sleeping in sunshine, she drifted away into sweet lethargy, drowning in him.

His hands slid round her body; one crept under her yellow sweater, moved inside her shirt to caress her breasts, his light touch making her flesh ache and swell, rounding into his palm. The other hand stroked down over the slim hips in their close-fitting jeans. The zip slid down and she stiffened, her eyes opening wide in shock.

'Don't do that!'

Too late; his hand was inside her jeans, pushing down her brief panties, between her thighs, his fingers exploring deeper, making her burn and gasp, trembling.

She broke away, turning to run, and tripped over one of the elegant little brocade and gilt chairs.

'Careful!' Domenico lunged to catch her, but was too late. She sprawled full-length across the thick-piled carpet.

Domenico went down on his knees beside her, his face urgent, anxious. 'Are you hurt?'

She shook her head, trying to get up.

'You could have broken a leg!' he muttered, frowning. 'Keep still, Saskia.'

He held her shoulders down on the carpet, leaning over her, and her heart began to beat rapidly, loudly. She gave a wordless murmur of protest, her lashes quivering against her flushed cheek.

His face came down towards her; she looked at his mouth and the fight drained out of her; she couldn't move. Her lips parted, she breathed as if she had been running. Why was she fighting when she loved him like this?

It suddenly seemed crazy to push away what she wanted so badly. It might be the last time. The words echoed in her head. The last time ... it hurt even to say it.

With a groan, she gave in; her head lifted to meet his mouth, her arms went round his neck.

She heard the thick murmur of triumph escape from him as his lips caught hers, heard the hammer of his heart above her as she clung, kissing him hungrily.

Saskia ran her hands into his thick, sleek hair, feeling the shape of his head, the moulding of the skull beneath that hair, the power of his nape under her fingertips.

Eyes shut, she was re-learning him, rediscovering him. There was a change; a tension, a tautness, in flesh and muscle, as in mind. Domenico was not the same, mentally or physically.

'Saskia ... Saskia ...' he whispered hoarsely, on top of her, his weight pressing her down into the carpet. She began to tremble violently, mouth dry.

They had made love hundreds of times before, yet this was new, this was different. They were neither of them the same person. Pain and grief, loss and self-discovery had altered both of them. Saskia felt like a virgin; she wanted him and yet she was afraid.

His knee nudged her thighs apart, he slid between them, lifted his head to look down at her, his eyes half closed, the grey glittering between pale lids, his face a mask of desire, skin stretched tight over his bones, his mouth apart, breathing so fast it sounded as if he was dying.

'It's been so long, Saskia ... I need you; from the first minute I saw you, I knew it was you I needed ...'

His hands were busy, tugging her jeans down; he pushed her sweater up, and then her shirt, his head burrowing between her breasts, his mouth hot on her flesh, muttering passionate words into her body.

He kicked his own jeans away and she felt their bare legs touching, the roughness of hair on his against the smoothness of her own.

Feverishly she held him down on her, hot and cold at the same time, shivering, burning.

With a hoarse cry he finally entered her and she arched to take him, her head back, her eyes shut, moaning through parted, dry lips. Their bodies merged into one driving movement; she couldn't believe the force of that need, that mounting hunger; her whole body was shuddering, shaking, as if it were being torn apart. She heard herself making wild, almost sobbing sounds; heard Domenico gasping; perspiration trickled down her back, between her breasts. All the loneliness and need of the last two years was exploding now into this moment, like imprisoned birds released, flying out into the endless blue sky, on and on and on...

Afterwards he lay on her as if he were dead, except that the sound of his tortured breathing was shaking her again, and he was trembling.

She had her arms round him still, but it was different now; she was comforting him, stroking his hair, his back, as if he were a child and she were his mother. He had had tears in his eyes. She had felt them, wet against her cheek, when he fell forward like someone dying, his last, long groan breathed out against her skin.

For a long time they lay in silence and she thought he was asleep in the end, but then he stirred, his cheek against hers.

'Saskia...my God, Saskia...I've dreamed of making love to you so often over the past two years, I'm afraid you'll vanish the way you do in my dreams; I'm afraid I'm going to wake up and find you gone again.'

Her heart wrenched inside her at the pain in his voice, the pain echoing inside his mind, his heart. She had hurt him far more than she had ever dreamt she would, or could.

When she had run away, she had believed he hated her, was bitterly angry with her, for losing her baby. Everyone around her had seemed an enemy, looking at her with the same cold contempt, accusing her. She had accused herself. She had lain awake night after night tortured by grief and fear and self-contempt.

She had hated herself for not being able to carry a child full-term. Every time she saw a woman with a pram Saskia had turned white, full of envy and misery. Other women have babies, why can't I? she had brooded. She had despised herself; it was easy to believe Domenico despised her, too. It was all she deserved. Looking back now, she saw that she had been half crazy—all the pressures of her marriage to Domenico had piled up on top of each other: his family's hostility, the contempt of the servants, her miscarriage and the depression she went into afterwards.

She and Domenico hadn't come closer together after the miscarriage. If anything they had turned away from each other; they had stopped talking. She had been given tranquillisers to help her sleep, and Domenico had moved out of their room. The pills she took had made her feel as if her head was full of cotton wool, made her feel unreal.

No wonder depression had turned into a nervous breakdown. Isolated, almost paranoid, the shadows had closed in on her.

She hadn't really been aware of what anyone else was feeling—until the moment when her father-in-law broke down and attacked her, and then the darkness around her had turned into a nightmare and she had fled.

Only now did it dawn on her that she had never once tried to reach Domenico, find out how he was suffering—grief had made her selfish; she should have tried to talk to him, tried to comfort him, because he had been grieving, too; he had needed her, just as she had needed him. She had picked up his emotions, his pain and rage, and turned them against herself; but she had been blind. Domenico's anger had not been directed at her, but at fate.

'We'll start again, darling, in a new place, with a new life; I've made sure that all the people who hurt you, all the reminders of what happened, have gone,' he whispered. 'From now on things will be different; this time it will work.'

She wanted to cry. How could she tell him, after the way they had just made love, that she could never bear to come back to him, could never bear to risk such suffering again?

What was she to say to him?

While she was struggling with words, the silence was broken by a vibrating, purring, whirring sound outside in the sky.

Domenico stiffened, lifting his head, listening. 'The helicopter!' he muttered. 'I'd forgotten all about it!'

Saskia sat up, trembling, clouds of auburn hair across her face, masking her expression from him. She grabbed up her clothes and began to dress with hands that shook.

Domenico dressed too. She didn't look at him but she was intensely conscious of that half-naked body, supple, powerful. If only they had had more time—if only life hadn't immediately begun to break in upon their few moments together.

She had to leave him again, but this time it was going to hurt far more. She hadn't learnt to love him less during their two years apart. Just now she had discovered that. She loved him more now. Leaving him was going to be agony.

Getting up, she huskily muttered, 'I'd like to use your downstairs cloakroom before we go.'

'You know where it is!' he said, buttoning his shirt.

She had used it before lunch, an elegant room, all creamy marble and glass, very modern, yet in keeping with the Renaissance architecture. She stood in front of the mirrors, her reflection showing a flushed, troubled face, her blue eyes full of confusion and uncertainty.

Fiercely she began to comb her dark auburn hair into some sort of shape. She couldn't face Giovanni looking as if she had been dragged through a hedge backwards. This meeting was going to be enough of an ordeal as it was.

Domenico was waiting for her in the hall. He was immaculate again, his hair brushed, his face cool. He ran a glance down over her, grinned teasingly.

'Don't worry, no one looking at us will guess what we've been doing!'

Ignoring that, she asked, 'Where will the helicopter land? Is it far away?'

'No, the landing pad is a short walk up behind the house.'

The spring afternoon sunshine was surprisingly hot when they left the house. Saskia wished she had thought to bring sunglasses; the light dazzled her; she couldn't bear to look up at the sky.

There were two bodyguards standing outside on the lawn, their eyes constantly moving, on the watch for any unexpected arrivals. As she and Domenico walked past, the other two men split up, one walking in front, the other behind.

Saskia shivered. She hated this feeling of being watched all the time, never being alone.

The helicopter blades were still whirring round as they came towards the landing pad. The machine looked like a giant green insect poised for a mighty leap.

'Keep your head down, and don't straighten up,' warned Domenico.

They ran, bent double, but suddenly someone inside the helicopter swung round to face them and Saskia saw the glint of the sun on metal, heard a burst of noise that froze her in her tracks.

Domenico's hand hit her violently in the back, knocking her down flat; he came down with her, fell on top of her, pushing her face into the ground.

Half smothered, gasping, she didn't understand what was happening; she heard the insistent rattle of what she suddenly knew was automatic rifle fire, she heard other shots, the handguns of the bodyguards, she realised, shouting, cries of pain, then a brief silence. For a second everything was still; she heard alarm calls of birds, the rustle of the grass.

Then a voice shouted in hoarse Italian.

'You! Alessandros! Get up, get in here! Unless you want your head blown off!'

Saskia felt Domenico stiffen, then he got up. She tried to get up too, but he muttered through his teeth to her.

'Stay down! Don't move!'

'Who's she?' the hoarse voice demanded.

'Nobody,' Domenico said. 'My secretary.'

'Domenico!' Saskia screamed, getting up on her knees.

He was being dragged into the helicopter. She saw two men in the cabin, one in a helmet and dark-glass visor, completely unrecognisable, the other on his knees, facing Domenico, pulling some sort of black cloth bag over Domenico's head, tying it loosely around the throat.

Saskia screamed. The gunman swung round and the black automatic weapon pointed at her.

As he opened fire she flung herself down on the ground instinctively and the burst of fire passed over her head. The noise of the engine grew louder, the machine was taking off; she heard Domenico yell her name in anguish.

Inside her head his voice echoed even louder. 'Saskia! Saskia! Did he hit you? Are you hurt?'

She lay very still, face down in the grass, eyes shut, her whole body tensed, all her energy narrowed to a tiny focus, sending a message back. 'I'm OK…he missed…'

She felt the lift of his relief.

The grass around her blew wildly, green stalks stirring against her face. The sound of the helicopter engine was starting to move away. She lifted her head and saw the dark green shape against the blue sky, flying quite low, heading west.

Shaking, tears running down her face, she scrambled to her knees and on to her feet.

That was when she saw the two bodyguards, sprawled face down on the grass a few yards away. Neither of them moved. Red blood spread across the back of one. The other's hair was matted with the same wet, dark stain.

Only then did the full horror of what had happened come home to Saskia, and terror welled up inside her.

CHAPTER SEVEN

SOMEBODY came crashing through laurel bushes behind her. Saskia swung, sobbing, a scream choked in her throat.

She was so screwed up that she didn't even recognise Pietro for a second.

Flushed, breathing heavily, he came to a halt, saw her, gave a quick look around and saw the two men sprawled unmoving on the grass. He looked quickly from them back to Saskia.

'Are you OK?'

She nodded.

Pietro ran to the two bodyguards, knelt beside the nearest one, put a roughened hand against his neck, pressing down into the vein.

'He's dead, isn't he?' Saskia whispered.

'No, he's alive. He was hit in the shoulder and back, there are two wounds here; I don't think either of them will be fatal,' Pietro said over his shoulder, getting up.

Saskia knew she should do something but she was shaking so much, she couldn't move at all. Her tongue seemed too big for her mouth. She swallowed and said thickly, 'They took him...Domenico...my husband...they took him.'

Pietro had gone over to the man with the gunshot wound to the head.

He didn't react to what she'd said.

'This one is in a very bad way; head wounds are always worse,' he said, then fished inside the bodyguard's pocket, pulled out a radio phone, tapped in a number, talked into the phone.

116

He had already worked out what had happened, Saskia thought. As soon as he saw the bodyguards he knew.

She looked up into the empty sky. The helicopter had vanished. Domenico had vanished.

What were they going to do with him? She was so cold. She wished she could stop shaking.

She suddenly picked up what Pietro was saying. 'I didn't see anything, just the helicopter coming in to land, then I heard gunfire, automatic rifle... I ran to the landing pad but when I got here it was all over; the chopper had gone, and Mr Alessandros had been snatched.' He paused, listening. 'Oh, five minutes ago? Couldn't be more. I ran as soon as I heard the firing; I saw the chopper take off. It was heading west.' Another pause. 'Yes, west from here.'

He must be talking to the police, thought Saskia. Of course. It was vital to get them looking for that helicopter as soon as possible. After all, the helicopter had to land somewhere. It needed the right sort of terrain for a landing. It couldn't just disappear the way a car could. People noticed helicopters where they might not notice cars. The police could catch up with whoever had taken Domenico if they knew soon enough that he had been kidnapped. The police had helicopters. If they could track the kidnappers before they landed they would have a chance. Once the helicopter had landed it would be far too easy for the men in it to disappear in cars, taking Domenico with them.

Pietro was still talking.

'Mrs Alessandros is with me; she's unharmed, but we need an ambulance for two men who have been badly shot up. No, both alive, but it's urgent we get them to a hospital as soon as possible.' Another pause, then he nodded. 'No, we haven't moved them. Yes. I'll wait here with them, and send Mrs Alessandros down to the house.'

He closed down the phone and looked at Saskia. 'An ambulance will be on the way here at once, and the police will be on their way too. I think it would be best for you to go down to the house, but you mustn't go alone; I'll ring my wife and ask her to come and get you. Try to remember everything you can about the men who took your husband—any little detail could be useful.'

Saskia remembered everything, but she was concentrating instead on Domenico, sending her thoughts to him, wondering if they would still be able to make contact when they were so far apart.

Are you OK? Domenico, are you OK? she thought. Can you hear me? Domenico. Answer me.

For a moment she thought it wasn't going to work, then she heard his voice as if he were whispering in her ear.

Don't worry. Stay calm, Saskia.

She gave a stifled sob. How could she stay calm when his life was in danger?

What are they going to do to you? she asked him, but this time she got no answer back, although she felt sure he had picked up her thoughts. He wasn't answering, though.

Why wasn't he? Did he know what his captors intended to do with him? She shuddered, her stomach clenched in fear.

Pietro was talking on the phone again, this time to his wife. 'You heard it too? Leo and Enrico have been shot. No, not dead, but they're both bad. The boss was taken. Who knows? Could be anyone. If it's for ransom they'll be in touch, we'll have to wait. Can you come up here and help Mrs Alessandros? And bring some blankets.' His voice lowered, almost to a whisper; he was turning away from Saskia, murmuring into the phone. 'As white as a ghost and she's hardly said a thing. I guess she's in shock. She saw it all. No, she wasn't shot, but she looks as if she doesn't know what time of day it is.'

He closed the phone again and turned back to Saskia. 'My wife is coming at once. You ought to lie down, Mrs

Alessandros. The police will want to talk to you, then we'll get a doctor to give you something to help you sleep.'

'No!' The last thing she wanted to do was sleep. She needed to be awake, to be ready to pick up any message Domenico might send her.

She felt Pietro watching her warily. 'Now, you be sensible...I know how you must feel, but it won't help your husband for you to be living on your nerves!'

'I'll be fine,' she said obstinately.

They both heard someone running towards them, feet thudding; they turned, but it wasn't Pietro's wife, it was the two bodyguards who had followed Jamie and Adriano to Venice and were now back.

They took in the scene at a glance. 'Where's the boss? What the hell has happened here?'

It was Pietro who answered.

'He sent for the chopper, but someone got to the pilot before he took off. They just found him, out cold, gagged and tied up. He didn't see who hit him. The police were just going to ring through here when I rang them.'

'You've already talked to the police?'

Pietro nodded.

'They're coming?'

Pietro nodded again.

The man who had been shot in the back moved weakly, began moaning. One of the other bodyguards went over to kneel down and pat him lightly on the arm, muttered soothingly.

'You're going to be OK, Leo. Don't worry. Just a flesh wound. We'll get you to hospital as soon as we can.'

The other asked Pietro, 'Who was here when Leo and Giorgio were hit? You?'

Pietro shook his head. His eyes slid sideways to touch on Saskia.

'Mrs Alessandros was the only one who saw what happened.'

The two bodyguards looked at her, eyes hard and suspicious.

'The police said to leave it to them to talk to her,' Pietro told them, and their faces settled like drying concrete.

'You'd better take her to the house. Oh, and bring some blankets up here!'

'My wife's bringing some up now.' But Pietro touched Saskia's arm, to attract her attention.

She started, her blue eyes wide, darkened with the intensity of her concentration on trying to reach Domenico.

'I'll walk down with you, Mrs Alessandros,' Pietro said.

Like an automaton she walked down the grassy slope beside him. It was strange to feel the heat of the sun on her neck and back. Her skin was so icy; the sun couldn't warm it back to life.

They met Pietro's wife a moment later. She handed a pile of blankets to Pietro, whispered to him, shaking her head in dismay, gave Saskia a quick look then put her arm around Saskia's shoulders in a motherly way.

'Come and lie down; I'll get Adriano's wife to make you a pot of English tea. That's what the English like to drink when they're upset, isn't it? Tea.'

'The police want to talk to her, so don't give her any sedatives or let her go off to sleep yet,' Pietro said, low-voiced.

His wife nodded.

Pietro moved off with the blankets back to the landing pad, and his wife guided Saskia down to the house.

Adriano met them at the door, his face pale and shocked. 'This is terrible, terrible,' he said to Saskia, who looked at him, shivering.

'Could your wife make her some tea? I'll stay with her,' Pietro's wife said.

She took Saskia upstairs to the main bedroom. Saskia stood in the middle of the room, picking up Domenico's vibrations stronger here than ever. This was his room. She closed her eyes and could feel him in here.

She walked over to the dressing-table and touched his silver hairbrush, ran her palm over the bristles, picked a long black hair from between them, wound it round her index finger while Pietro's wife watched her, frowning, perplexed.

'Why don't you lie down, my dear? You look terrible. Take off your shoes and lie down. It will be OK, you'll see. They won't harm him; he's too valuable to them alive.'

For the moment, thought Saskia. Sickness welled inside her. Even if the ransom was paid would they let him go? How many times had she read about kidnappings where the victim was killed even though the ransom was paid? Killed so that he couldn't identify his kidnappers or where he had been held?

Don't! a voice inside her head ordered. Don't think like that!'

She stared at nothing. Domenico! Where are you?

'Come along, my dear, lie down,' Pietro's wife pleaded, anxiously watching her set white face, and Saskia gave in, lay down on the bed, her head pillowed where Domenico's head usually lay, staring at the window, the blue sky which had swallowed him up such a short time ago.

Mrs Baldacci covered her with a continental quilt which was very light, yet very warm. Her body was shuddering helplessly, her teeth chattering. She gave a long sigh as the warmth of the quilt enveloped her.

Mrs Baldacci hovered, watching her. Saskia could hear the clock ticking, could hear the other woman breathing. She wished she could stop shaking.

From outside they heard the sound of motorboats down on the canal, then loud voices, people running up the steps to the house.

Mrs Baldacci went to the window, peered down. 'It's the ambulancemen, and the police,' she said. 'They've got here quickly.

Adriano came up with a tray, beautifully laid with an embroidered white cloth, a silver teapot, a cup and saucer made of porcelain so fine that you could see through it. He poured tea, added milk, sugar, stirred it, bent over Saskia with the cup.

'Shall I put it on the table for you, *signora*? Or will you sit up and drink it at once while it is hot?'

She didn't care. But she saw he wanted her to drink the tea so she sat up and took the cup and saucer from him. They rattled in her shaking hands. She lifted the cup to her lips, holding it between her palms. The warmth of the china was comforting.

The tea was just hot enough to drink; as it ran down her throat she felt her body reacting to the sudden warmth, the intake of sugar she was so desperately needing to fight the shock.

Someone tapped on the door and Adriano went over to open it; she heard a low murmur of voices, then Adriano turned and looked at her uncertainly.

'Will you talk to the police now, *signora*?'

She nodded eagerly, put her cup and saucer down on the table beside the bed as two men came into the room.

Their dark eyes flicked around, from Saskia to Mrs Baldacci, back to Adriano.

One was a tall man in his thirties, tall, slim, with smooth, slicked-back hair. The other was shorter, with pudgy features and the look of a bulldog, a snub nose, jowls, a sagging chin.

It was the tall man who took control. 'It would be easier if we talked to you alone, Mrs Alessandros,' he politely suggested, and the other man opened the door again, held it pointedly.

'Do you want me to stay with you, *signora*?' Mrs Baldacci asked Saskia, bristling, her face defiant.

Saskia smiled faintly at her, shook her head. 'I'll be OK, thank you.'

Reluctantly, Mrs Baldacci left and so did Adriano after a pause. The door closed and the tall policeman took a chair and sat down beside the bed, crossed his legs, gave a routine smile to Saskia.

'I am Captain Rosi. This is Lieutenant Angelo. I'm in charge of this investigation for the moment. Tell us exactly what happened, Mrs Alessandros. Try to remember everything you can; every tiny detail could be useful.'

She flatly went through the story from the minute that she and Domenico walked up to the landing pad.

'Can you describe either of the men in the helicopter?'

'The pilot was wearing a helmet with a smoked-glass visor that covered the top of his face, so I couldn't see much of him.'

'You must have noticed something about him!'

'His mouth was thin; I think he had a moustache, a small, fine moustache. I got the impression he was in his twenties, maybe a bit older.'

'Build?'

'Slim. I couldn't tell his height, he was sitting down, but I don't think he was very tall. The other man...the one with the gun...was older, he was thickset, he had dark glasses on, his nose was fleshy, his mouth was full, very red, he was very tanned.' She concentrated harder. 'I saw his hands...he was wearing black gloves, leather gloves...but he had a bracelet on one wrist, a gold identity bracelet.'

The other man was recording what she said on a small, portable tape recorder, and writing it down in a notebook at the same time.

The younger man listened, his foot swinging. He wore shiny, well-polished black boots and was in the *carabinieri* uniform; immaculate, formidable.

'Tell me again what was said,' he asked and she repeated everything she could remember.

'I gather you and your husband have been separated for some time,' he asked politely, his face expressionless.

She nodded. 'For two years.'

'So why are you here today?'

'I was staying in Venice, and ran into my husband, and he invited us ... that is, myself and the friend I was with ... to visit this house. I'd never seen it before; we used to live in Milan; my husband inherited this house since I left him.'

'And your friend? Male or female, by the way?'

She got the impression he already knew the answer to that.

'Male—Jamie Forster; he's not so much a friend as my boss; I work in his garden centre in England. He left immediately after lunch. He was taken back to Venice by Adriano and two of my husband's bodyguards. I was going to visit my father-in-law, with my husband.'

He considered her. 'An odd coincidence ...'

She was bewildered. 'What is?'

'That the day you visited your husband for the first time after an absence of two years was the very day that somebody staged a kidnap attempt and snatched Mr Alessandros.'

She stared, pale and incredulous. 'You don't think I had anything to do with this?'

It hadn't even occurred to her that anyone would suspect she might be involved in the kidnap of Domenico.

'At this stage of the investigation I don't have any fixed ideas, Mrs Alessandros. I was just making an observation. Don't you think it a strange coincidence?' He sounded polite but his eyes were sharp, distrustful.

'That's all it is. A coincidence.' She couldn't believe they actually suspected her! 'Why would I want my husband kidnapped?'

'He's a very wealthy man. He comes from an old Catholic family; divorce would be out of the question and that means you can't get your freedom. If you've met someone else and want to marry again, that could be a very powerful motive.'

'I haven't met anyone else! And even if I had, if I wanted to divorce him in my own country, I could. Under our laws, I would simply have to wait five years, that's all. I don't need his agreement to a divorce after five years.'

'But you would not get a divorce settlement from Mr Alessandros, would you, in that case?'

'I wouldn't take any money from my husband! I can earn all the money I need.'

Both men stared at her.

'I wish my wife thought like that, don't you Lieutenant?' Captain Rosi murmured to his colleague who grinned.

'All the same, Mrs Alessandros, it is strange that your husband's bodyguards were shot, and he was snatched, but you came off unharmed,' the captain added drily. 'There seem to have been a number of odd coincidences—that you just happened to bump into your husband in Venice, that you were here with him alone when the helicopter arrived, that the kidnappers didn't either try to take you too, or shoot at you.'

'I've told you . . . Domenico . . . my husband told them that I was his secretary. He was trying to protect me. And they did shoot at me, but they missed.'

He smiled incredulously. 'They missed. Amazing luck for you. They seem to have had no trouble hitting the two bodyguards, do they?'

'The helicopter was taking off when the gunman fired at me.' Suddenly angry, she flushed and said, 'This is ridiculous. I tell you, I'm not behind this kidnap. I wouldn't harm a hair on Domenico's head! And how could I plan something like this? I don't even know where

the helicopter was coming from...it was my husband
who decided to call for the helicopter, out of the blue.
It hadn't been planned in advance. It was a sudden decision. He wanted to take me to see his father, who lives
just outside Padua.'

Captain Rosi studied her thoughtfully, eyes narrowed.
'It was a sudden decision? Not planned in advance?'

'No. My father-in-law rang up just before lunch, and
asked Domenico to take me to see him, so on the spur
of the moment Domenico suggested we go after lunch,
and he rang up his pilot.'

Snapping his fingers, the captain gestured to his colleague, who held out the notebook in which he had taken
down what she was saying.

The captain skimmed his eyes down the pages, his lips
pursed, humming tunelessly to himself. Then he looked
up again.

'You are sure the helicopter was flying westwards?'

'Yes. Hasn't anyone seen it? A helicopter can't just
vanish! Someone must have seen it flying overhead, or
seen it land!'

'It takes time to get in reports from eye-witnesses; we'll
undoubtedly hear something in due course. Now, Mrs
Alessandros, can we go back to what was actually said
during the kidnap...did you hear any names mentioned?'

'No,' she said, then frowned. 'But one thing...'

'Yes?' Captain Rosi was swinging his foot again; she
realised he did that when he was excited or on edge. She
watched his shiny black boots, half hypnotised by the
rhythmic movement.

Her voice was low, husky. 'They recognised my
husband because they spoke to him... "Alessandros!
Get up, get in here!" they said, so they must have known
what he looked like.'

'He is a well-known figure in Italy.'

She sighed. 'Yes, of course, that's true.'

'But they apparently didn't know you?'

She stared, confused. 'What?'

'You claim they asked who you were...'

'Oh.' She frowned. 'Yes, that's right, they said, "Who's she?" and Domenico said I was his secretary.' She broke off. 'No, he said, "Nobody. My secretary."'

Captain Rosi stared fixedly at her. 'He said, "Nobody. My secretary"?'

She nodded.

'So why did they try to shoot you? You did say they shot at you?'

She had to concentrate. 'I started to get up, that was it. I got up, and then I screamed. I said my husband's name, I think. I saw the man with the gun kneeling on his seat, turned round to face Domenico; he was putting a black bag over Domenico's head.'

'A black bag?'

'Like a shoe bag, the sort children take to school, with drawstrings at the neck.'

'Ah. Yes. Go on—what happened then?'

'When I screamed, he turned round and fired at me and as he did that I threw myself down again...it was just instinctive...the helicopter was taking off as he fired, too, and I think that spoilt his aim; it swung round and round for a second, and the firing went right over my head, then the helicopter was flying away, and I heard my husband asking if I was hurt; he was upset, and I told him I wasn't, I was OK.'

'You didn't mention this before.' The captain's eyes were flinty with suspicion again. He flipped over the notes his colleague had taken, found an earlier piece. 'I asked you to tell me everything that had been said, but you never mentioned your husband asking if you were hurt, or that you replied.'

She bit her lip. 'It wasn't...said...'

The man's brows lifted. 'What?'

'Not said, aloud,' she whispered.

He exchanged a look with his colleague. 'Not said aloud? What does that mean?'

She knew they wouldn't believe her. What was the point of trying to explain?

'Well, Mrs Alessandros?' Captain Rosi persisted and she sighed.

'My husband and I can...sometimes...read each other's mind.' She saw the man's face change, the pull of irritation at his lips, the disbelief in his eyes. 'It's true! We have...a...telepathic link, sometimes; it doesn't always work, but if he's angry, or upset, or afraid...I can sometimes pick up what he's feeling.'

'I see,' the man said drily. 'And can he pick up yours?'

'Yes, it works both ways.'

She hadn't known that until she discovered that Domenico was picking up her thoughts when they met in the Accademia art gallery; that instant of communication had changed everything between them, she saw that now. During the two years they had been apart, Domenico had been trying to reach her, anyhow, any way he could, and he had somehow tuned into her wavelength, but it had only really begun to work once they met again. With a sickening sense of fear she wondered if it only worked if they were close to each other. What if they were miles apart? Would the link break?

The lieutenant said in a carefully patient voice with an undertone of mockery, 'OK, then, Mrs Alessandros—why don't you give us a demonstration? Can you contact him now and ask where he is?'

The bland voice, the veiled eyes, the secret amusement did not escape her, but she didn't care what this man thought, whether he believed her or not. She needed to get into touch with Domenico; she wanted to know that he was still alive, still safe, unharmed.

With quiet dignity, she said, 'I'll try, but I need to concentrate; you must be quiet—don't speak to me, or interrupt me.'

'What happens if someone speaks to you? You have a fit? Is that it? Turn into ectoplasm, or something?' His mockery was out in the open now. He was grinning. No doubt he thought she was crazy, talking utter nonsense.

'Make fun of me if you like, Captain Rosi. But it's very simple—if I don't concentrate, shut out everything else around me, I won't be able to tune into Domenico. You understand that the air is full of radio waves, don't you? You believe in television and telephones—you're happy to accept that you can see what's happening right now in London, by simply switching on the TV, so what's so unbelievable about human thought being transmitted through the air waves too?'

Captain Rosi stared at her, his face blank, then got up. 'Well, I think we'll go down and talk to the servants and bodyguards while you're trying to "tune in", then, Mrs Alessandros. We'll leave you quite alone to do that. Come along, Angelo.'

They went out and she heard them laughing on the landing, then their boots thudding on the marble floors as they went downstairs.

No, they didn't believe a word of what she had said. But she didn't care. All she cared about was Domenico.

Saskia lay flat on the bed, her eyes closed, her whole being concentrated towards him, wherever he was. He could be miles away by now, and whatever communication they had built up might not operate across such a distance.

But she wasn't going to stop trying. Just in case something could get through.

She lost all sense of time, except that she knew the room was darkening around her; it was twilight, night was coming on and the temperature was dropping. In spite of the quilt covering her, Saskia was cold; she kept shivering.

Suddenly she sensed Domenico shivering too. He was even colder than she.

Cold. And dark, she thought. He is cold and in the dark. She drew a stark breath.

She had reached him.

Dark, his mind was telling her. Cold. Dark. No, he wasn't saying he was in the dark. Blind! He was telling her he was blind; he couldn't see at all.

For a second panic went through her, then she remembered. They had put a hood over his head. It must still be there.

Domenico, can you hear me? she asked him.

He didn't answer, but she knew she was in tune with him—her mind was locked in with his; she was experiencing what was happening to him.

He wasn't in the helicopter any more. They had landed somewhere. She circled in her mind, casting around, like a hunting dog trying to pick up a scent, but she couldn't work out in which direction they had flown.

But they had landed, she was sure of that. Domenico had been bundled into the boot of a car. He was being bumped about, rolling helplessly with every swerve, every corner the vehicle took.

He couldn't see a thing, but he could hear the revving of the engine. The driver was in a tearing hurry. They were driving very fast, over rough, badly made up roads.

Mountain roads, she thought? Yes, winding, steep mountain roads with ruts in them. Every time they went over a bad patch Domenico was thrown about; he was bruised and aching already.

The car slowed. Stopped. She heard wind blowing fiercely; grass rustling, the sound of sheep bells somewhere, and closer at hand the bleating of an animal…not a sheep. No, not a sheep. A goat, she decided.

The boot of the car was being opened. Domenico was being dragged out, manhandled and pushed along a flinty path; rough grass, gorse, thistles brushed past his legs.

He was thrown through a doorway and fell; his head hit a stone wall.

The images stopped. It was as if a television had been switched off. Suddenly there was nothing coming through.

Saskia sat up, a hand at her mouth, gasping a sob.

Domenico had been knocked out when his head hit that wall.

She rolled off the bed and ran across the room, opened the door and looked down the stairs.

Captain Rosi was talking to Adriano and his wife in the hall. They all looked up, stared at Saskia.

She leaned over the banisters. Her voice shaking, she said, 'They've landed; they've driven up into the mountains.'

There was a thick silence; she saw their faces with a sinking heart and knew they weren't ready to listen or believe her.

'Italy's full of mountains,' said the captain. 'Which ones would these be?'

'I don't know,' she had to admit. 'Domenico doesn't know, so he can't tell me. They locked him into the boot of the car they were driving; and anyway, he can't see, he's still hooded; he can't tell me where he is.'

'But he did mention that it was in the mountains?' Captain Rosi said with soft sarcasm, smiling.

'Oh, why won't you listen to me?' Saskia burst out in anguish. 'Why should I lie to you? I want to help you find my husband—I'm afraid. I'm scared that they may be going to kill him.'

Captain Rosi took that seriously enough. He came up the stairs towards her, frowning. 'What makes you think they'll do that?'

'I just felt them drag Domenico from the boot of that car, shove him along a rough path and throw him against a stone wall. The way they're treating him makes me sure they mean to kill him!'

There was a heavy silence. The captain stared fixedly at her white face, the tears running down it.

Angry with herself for giving way to emotions in front of a man who clearly distrusted everything she said or did, Saskia put a hand up to brush them away.

As she did so the front door opened and a uniformed officer came in with some new arrivals. Everyone turned to look at them.

Saskia's heart leapt.

'Anna!' she cried out, pushing past Captain Rosi and running down the stairs. 'Anna, thank God you've come!'

CHAPTER EIGHT

ANNA opened her arms and Saskia ran into them; they hugged, both in tears.

'Oh, Saskia, this is terrible news!' Anna's voice was softer, warmer, yet in other ways she was so like her brother; they had always been closer, the two of them, than Domenico had been with his other sisters; perhaps that was why Anna had been the one who was ready to accept Saskia when Domenico brought her home.

'It was all so fast, I still can't believe it!' Saskia looked at Anna's dark hair and grey eyes, read Domenico in her face and was moved unbearably. 'You got here fast; were you in Milan? How did you do it so quickly?'

'We were in Padua, visiting Papà—we were waiting, expecting you and Domenico, when the news came—it was such a shock!'

Saskia looked sharply at her. 'You didn't tell your father? A shock like that could kill him.'

'No, of course not; just said you had been delayed and would come tomorrow, then we made an excuse and left. The staff at the nursing home will make sure he doesn't see the TV tonight, or see any papers tomorrow.'

Saskia bit her lip. 'Domenico didn't tell me you would be at Padua.'

Anna sobbed. 'It was to be a surprise. He told us you were coming. I was so excited. Oh, Saskia...what actually happened? Were you there?'

Saskia nodded grimly, told her in short, husky sentences, then broke off and said, 'I'm so afraid, Anna. These men are brutal...' She stopped again, pulled free of her sister-in-law, looked at Captain Rosi, who had

133

come downstairs to join them, and said in a quiet voice, 'Anna, will you tell this man that I am telepathic? He doesn't believe me.'

Anna's dark eyes searched hers. 'You've been reading Nico's mind? Ahh... yes, of course, you always could, I remember.' She looked at the captain, nodding vehemently. 'It's true, Captain—she can.'

Captain Rosi's face took on the familiar indulgent amusement. 'I'm afraid we can't use party games in police work, Signora Monfalcone.'

Anna's olive skin flushed angrily. 'I'm not talking about games, Captain! Saskia is telepathic, genuinely telepathic; she can pick things out of the air. If she says she has read my brother's mind, believe her.'

Her elegantly dressed, comfortably built husband moved close to her, as though silently conveying his support, and the captain looked from one to the other of them.

The telephone was ringing. Captain Rosi snapped his fingers at one of his men, who hurried off to answer it.

'Go back to bed, Mrs Alessandros,' he said quite gently. 'You should be resting. I'll get a doctor to see you, prescribe a sedative, to help you sleep.'

'No, I'm not taking sedatives, I must stay awake, in case...' She broke off as the man who had answered the phone came back, looking excited.

'Sir! Headquarters, they want to talk to you. They've located the chopper; it's been abandoned...'

'Where?' Saskia burst out.

Captain Rosi scowled at the junior officer. 'I'll come and talk to them.' He turned to Anna. 'Perhaps you will take care of your sister-in-law, Signora Monfalcone.'

He strode away and Anna angrily looked at her husband. 'Guido! The man's rude and a fool. Talk to him!'

Guido grimaced. 'When I get a chance I'll have a word, my love, but let's try diplomacy before we go to war, shall we? You take Saskia upstairs and talk to her, I'll see what I can do with the captain in my own way. We don't yet know precisely what is going on; it might be more sensible to wait until we know more.'

He walked away towards the big salon and Anna gazed after him with a fulminating expression.

'Men! What can you do with even the best of them? He's going to get himself a drink and sit down and wait, then he and the captain will have a drink together and talk about what silly little things women are, and maybe eventually Guido will say, Look, old chap, humour them, will you? Just for a quiet life! And that's what he calls diplomacy.'

'I don't care how Guido does it, so long as he can persuade Captain Rosi to listen to me. Domenico's life may depend on it!' Her voice broke on a stifled sob.

Anna put an arm round her. 'Come upstairs, Saskia. The captain is right about one thing—you do need to rest. You look terrible, I'm afraid. As white as a peeled onion.'

Saskia put a foot on the bottom stair and then stopped, her face stiffening, whiter than ever, her eyes dark and fixed.

Anna looked sharply at her, opened her mouth, shut it again, waited.

Saskia had heard Domenico inside her head. But he hadn't been calling her. Anguish stabbed in her chest.

Claudia! he was saying. Claudia!

The name brought an instant image with it—Claudia Forli, who had been his secretary for years; dark hair, dark eyes, a sensual woman with full red lips and a body that made men stare.

Saskia had always been jealous of her, but Domenico had insisted that he had never been interested in Claudia sexually.

Obviously he had lied. He was saying her name now with a force that made Saskia's heart hurt. Over and over again he kept saying it—he sounded as if he was in pain, and calling out for Claudia.

Tears pricked under her lids; she took a stumbling step upwards. She couldn't bear it. Domenico and Claudia...well, hadn't she always wondered, suspected, been afraid? She began to run up the stairs, sobbing, and then stopped again as Domenico's voice spoke fiercely inside her head.

Saskia...oh, God, am I getting through to you? Saskia...concentrate, concentrate, darling. She felt as if he took a deep breath, then she heard him thinking again. Saskia . . . listen . . . Saskia . . . tell them Claudia...Claudia Forli, Saskia...

The voice faded again and Saskia turned a dazed, confused face on Anna, staring, wide-eyed at her.

'What is it?' Anna demanded, staring back at her, dismayed by the way she looked.

'It was Domenico,' Saskia slowly said. 'But I don't understand what he means.'

She turned back and went down to the hall with Anna following her, frowning anxiously.

'What are you talking about, Saskia? I think you really should lie down; you're in shock, you know. You should rest. It won't do Domenico any good for you to make yourself ill; it won't help find him.'

Saskia walked into the salon where Guido was lounging on a chair, a glass in his hand, talking to Captain Rosi. Both men got up as she came into the room. The captain's black brows met and he scowled, the expression so familiar to her by now that she almost laughed.

'I thought you had gone to bed, Signora Alessandros.'

Calmly, she told him, 'My husband wants me to tell you something.'

'Oh, not again!' His voice rose angrily. 'Please, Signor Monfalcone, can't you make sure your sister-in-law goes to her room and stays there? I cannot have my investigation interrupted every five minutes with this talk of mind-reading—I'm not interested in any of that stuff, not telepathy, not table-tapping, not tarot-reading. Police work is done on purely rational methods. We gather information. We check and double-check all of it. We'll find Signor Alessandros, but we'll do it our way, not with the help of the spirit world!'

'Claudia Forli,' Saskia said. 'Domenico said to tell you: Claudia Forli.'

Through his teeth, Captain Rosi asked, 'I see. And who is Claudia Forli?'

'She used to work for my husband,' Saskia said. 'She got married and stopped working for him; that's all I know.'

Captain Rosi threw his hands up. 'And what am I supposed to do? Track her down and ask her if she has kidnapped your husband?'

Guido was on his feet. He put his glass down carefully, cleared his throat.

'Captain, Claudia Forli married a Sardinian...'

The captain's head turned sharply. 'A Sardinian?'

Guido met his eyes, nodded. In the silence they all thought the same thing. Kidnapping was a way of life in Sardinia for some of the poorer families, almost a traditional pursuit.

'Met him on holiday there, last summer. He was working in the hotel, teaching snorkelling, but I have a feeling Domenico told me the fellow came from the mountains, his family were shepherds.'

'Oh, were they?' Captain Rosi said, and now his entire attitude had changed.

'Some of those mountain people are involved in the kidnapping trade, aren't they?' asked Guido innocently. 'Mind you, it doesn't mean that Claudia's husband came from a family like that. But she married him much too fast; indecent haste, it seemed to me—hardly knew the fellow, after all. But then Claudia could probably hear her biological clock ticking away, poor woman; thirty-five, not much time left if she wanted a baby. I have a feeling she left her job because she was pregnant.' His face was cynical. 'Maybe this fellow married her for that reason, too. A holiday romance; she might have tried to get pregnant to force his hand.'

'I suppose you wouldn't happen to know this Sardinian's name?' asked the captain.

Guido shook his head. 'But I've no doubt my brother-in-law's office could give it to you. When Claudia married him it would have been put on her file and even though she left the firm her file will still be held; sometimes staff come back, you know.'

'And another thing,' Anna said. 'Claudia had a thing about my brother for years; she was always trying to get his attention. When he married Saskia it was a terrible shock for her. Then he and Saskia split up and I think Claudia hoped again for a while, but Domenico simply wasn't interested in her. Around that time she changed; even before she met this man on holiday in Sardinia, she was very bitter, always making sarcastic remarks, upsetting the other staff. And she started being un-punctual; half the time she was late for work in the mornings, took too long over lunch, she wasn't doing her job properly. If she hadn't resigned, Domenico was talking about sacking her.'

'I'll have her looked into at once,' Captain Rosi said and left the room.

Saskia was leaning on a chair-back, visibly trembling. Guido looked at his wife, shook his head, gestured to Saskia. Anna nodded and put her arm round Saskia's waist.

'Come on, bed for you.'

Upstairs she lay down like a child and Anna covered her with the quilt. Saskia closed her eyes; the room was quiet and warm, shadowy, just one lamp switched on at the other side of the room where Anna was sitting reading a magazine. Saskia listened to the quietness. Nothing came through from Domenico. She drifted off into a sleep-like rest, her body limp.

A tap on the door made her start up, but it wasn't news of Domenico, just the doctor that Captain Rosi had sent for.

'I don't need a doctor!' she protested.

'I just want to check that you are coping with the shock of all this,' the young man soothed, taking her pulse, his quick eyes noticing her pallor, the dark rings under her eyes, her dilated pupils.

'I'm fine!'

He smiled. 'I'd just like to take your blood-pressure, *signora*.'

Restlessly she permitted it. 'I'm not taking any sedatives. I don't want to go to sleep.'

He kept on smiling. 'I'm not going to prescribe a sleeping pill. But I would like you to take a tranquilliser to help you stay calm; that can't hurt, can it?'

'I think it's a very good idea,' Anna chimed in.

Saskia reluctantly agreed to take the two pills he handed her, swallowed them with some water, lay down again.

'And it would help if you undressed,' the doctor said with wry humour. 'You would feel more comfortable, *signora*. Now, if you need me again, you only have to ring. Goodnight, *signora*, and I'll pray that you have good news before morning.'

When he had gone Anna coaxingly asked, 'Will you put on a nightie?'

'I haven't got one with me.'

'Your clothes are all here,' Anna said, shocking her. 'Didn't Nico tell you? Everything you left behind when you went away... he had it all packed up and brought here when he moved. They're in the next room. I'll get you a nightie, shall I? Or would you rather wear pyjamas?'

Slowly, Saskia said, 'Pyjamas, please.'

Anna hurried out and Saskia lay staring at the ceiling. Domenico had brought all her clothes here with him— he must have been so sure he was going to find her. Why hadn't he told her this, when he was showing her round the house? He had briefly showed her the room next to his bedroom, but he hadn't said that it was full of her clothes. Tears stung her eyes. There had been so many misunderstandings, so much stupid pride and words unsaid.

Anna came back with peach silk pyjamas and a warm wool robe in a matching colour. She helped Saskia undress and put them on, then slid her back into bed, like a nurse with a sick patient.

'Doesn't that feel better?'

'Yes, thank you.' Saskia smiled, but she couldn't relax. 'Will they tell us if there is any news?' she fretted. 'Something must have happened by now... Anna, could you go down and ask Guido if he's heard anything?'

Anna hesitated. 'I don't like to leave you alone, dear.'

'I'm fine, I promise, I'll stay in bed!'

Anna shrugged. 'OK, so long as you do promise!'

When she had gone Saskia closed her eyes and concentrated, but there was still nothing, a complete blank. She had a sudden terrified thought: what if Domenico was dead?

Shock iced her body. She was trembling violently. Oh, God, don't let him be dead! she prayed, eyes still shut.

Of course, he could be asleep. It was dark outside now; night had fallen. Domenico had had a series of shocks today; he must be exhausted. She sighed heavily. Yes, that was probably it.

She wouldn't go to sleep, she would just rest, with her eyes closed, until Anna got back with some news. She wasn't sleepy, anyway, she wasn't at all tired...

She opened her eyes a little while later, yawning, and with a pang of shock realised that she must have drifted off, she had been asleep. The room was full of daylight, pale lavender dawn light, with a growing warmth to it as the sun came up and turned the morning golden.

Saskia sat up, was about to get out of bed when she caught sight of Anna in the full-length mirror on the opposite wall.

Anna was stretched out fast asleep on a *chaise-longue* at the end of the carved oak bed. She was covered with a duvet, but was still fully dressed. She looked pale, her hair tousled. Poor Anna! thought Saskia, watching her. She must be as worried about her brother as she, Saskia, was! I've been very selfish; I should have thought, put myself in Anna's place, realised how she was feeling. She has been so kind and thoughtful to me, a tower of strength, when she must have wanted to break down and cry, too.

Anna's lids fluttered, as if she had suddenly sensed she was being watched. They lifted; she stared up blankly at the ceiling, then gave a smothered groan as she moved stiffly, sat up, the duvet falling to the floor.

In the mirror she saw Saskia sitting in the bed. Saskia gave her a faint smile.

'You must be as stiff as a board, sleeping on that thing!'

Anna laughed, got up, rubbing her neck with one hand. 'I do feel as if I've been on the rack for a few hours! What about you? How are you?' She came over to the bed and studied Saskia wryly. 'Well, you have a little more colour, anyway.' Glancing at her watch, she grimaced. 'It's only six o'clock! I haven't been up this early for years. What I need is some coffee, good strong coffee. How about you?'

'Yes, please.'

Anna went out; Saskia swung out of the bed, put on her peach wool robe, felt the warmth envelop her. The dawn air was chilly. She went over to the window and looked out. There were shadowy figures in the grounds, down by the canal gate, armed *carabinieri*, in uniform, moving stiffly, after a night on guard. On the distant water bobbed several police boats; she saw a man on board one of them drinking from a large red china mug, the colour a bright dot in the mistiness veiling the canal.

Anna returned with Adriano, who carried a tray, loaded with coffee and rolls, black cherry jam, freshly squeezed orange juice.

'I found Adriano in the kitchen,' explained Anna. 'I don't think he's been to bed at all.'

Saskia gave him a concerned look. 'You should have gone to bed, Adriano; it won't help anyone for you to make yourself ill!'

'I don't sleep much, anyway, madam,' he reassured her.

Anna perched on the edge of the bed as he poured them both coffee. 'Lucky he didn't go to bed, actually— he eavesdropped on the captain's phone calls all night...'

Adriano bridled. 'I just happened to overhear the occasional call, *signora*!'

Anna grinned at him. 'Well, whatever! Anyway, what he overheard was very exciting—it seems that Claudia and her husband moved up into the Dolomites after she left.'

'The Dolomites!'

Anna nodded, eyes bright. 'Exactly—you can see them from the windows here, on clear days, right across the Po valley. I often ski up there; they have some wonderful resorts—I stay at Cortina d'Ampezzo; the scenery is magnificent. The actual mountains are an amazing colour—almost rose-pink at dawn and like a blood orange at sunset; I think the colour is something to do with the rocks being porphyry and limestone, although when they're covered in snow, of course, they're a sparkling white...'

'Anna, never mind what they look like!' erupted Saskia. 'If Claudia is living up in the mountains then maybe she and her husband are involved in kidnapping Domenico! Oh, surely it can't be Claudia...she isn't a criminal! And she did care for Domenico, I know she did; I knew from the minute I met her. She was so jealous she wanted to kill me.'

Anna made a face. 'I'm sure she did. And if you're looking for a motive...there it is! Jealousy, bitterness—come on, Saskia, use your head. Of course it could be Claudia.'

Saskia stared back at her, face drawn. 'One thing I can't understand is...why hasn't anybody got in touch, demanding a ransom?'

There was a silence; she caught the flicker of Anna's lashes and stiffened.

'Anna? Has there been a ransom demand?' She read the answer in Anna's face and took a sharp breath. 'There has, hasn't there? How much did they want? When did it come? Why wasn't I told?'

Anna sighed. 'I told Guido I couldn't keep secrets! They didn't want to tell you; Guido felt you were worried enough already. They found a ransom demand in the helicopter—stuck to the inside window, a huge sheet of paper scrawled in bright red lipstick, all capital letters.'

'How much?'

'I've no idea; the police prefer to keep the sum secret for the moment. Captain Rosi told us it would only the first demand, anyway, others would follow.'

Saskia couldn't stop shaking. 'Did they...make any...threats? About what they might do...to him? If the ransom wasn't paid?'

Anna shook her head, but Saskia wasn't sure she could believe the denial.

Her eyes darkened. 'Oh, God, I wish I knew what was really going on! I wish I knew what the *carabinieri* were doing. Where's Captain Rosi?'

'Local *carabinieri* will go up to Claudia's last address to check it out,' said Anna.

Adriano, his face very sombre, handed Saskia a cup of coffee. 'Please, sit down, *signora*; eat something—you haven't eaten for hours!'

She restlessly paced about, holding the hot coffee, half spilling it because her hands kept shaking.

'But... surely they wouldn't actually hold him at their own home? That would be stupid, and Claudia is not stupid.'

'The police have to start somewhere,' Anna pointed out. 'Sit down and eat, Saskia!'

With a groan, she obeyed. Anna spread a roll with cherry jam, gave it to her as if she were a child. Automatically she bit into it and as she did so felt her stomach clamour with hunger. It startled her. How could she want to eat when Domenico could be dead?

But she ate the roll, and drank the coffee, which was ambrosial; strong and thick. She accepted a second cup, began to feel rather more alive.

'Why don't you have a shower?' suggested Anna.

'I think I will, yes.'

'And remember, you have wardrobes full of beautiful clothes to change into! You can have a lot of fun rediscovering them all, like getting a whole new wardrobe all at once!' Anna grinned at Saskia, who managed a smile back.

'If they still fit me!'

Anna surveyed her frowningly. 'You have lost weight! Adriano, your wife must feed her up, so that she fits into all her old clothes!'

He smiled and Saskia laughed as she went off to have a shower. Twenty minutes later, feeling much more normal, scented with expensive talc and perfume, her auburn hair washed and blow-dried back into shape, she rejoined Anna downstairs, wearing a designer-made olive-green wool suit with a tight-fitting jacket under which she only wore a bra and silk chemise top, and a lightly flared skirt.

The two young uniformed officers in the hall watched her come down the stairs, their dark eyes appreciative of her slender figure, the fine black stockings, the delicate high heels.

Saskia hadn't worn anything like this for two years; she found herself enjoying the softness of the wool, the marvellous cut of the material. It had probably cost hundreds of pounds, judging by the label. She didn't remember how much the bill had come to. But she did remember how Domenico had looked when he saw her in it. He liked her to wear stylish clothes, and this suit had class.

She found Anna and Guido in the salon, talking. They had obviously showered and changed, too; they looked refreshed.

'Where's Captain Rosi?' she asked as they looked round, staring at her changed appearance.

'He left hours ago,' Guido said. 'You look ravishing, Saskia!'

'Thank you,' she said vaguely, her mind on what he had said. 'Where did the captain go? Has he gone to the Dolomites to help search for Domenico?'

Guido shrugged. 'He didn't say. He just went. Not a very talkative chap.'

Saskia froze suddenly, hearing a familiar sound outside in the sky, a sound that had chilled her blood yesterday, but which now sent a throb of hope through her.

'A helicopter!'

Anna and Guido went towards the window to look out, but Saskia was already running, back through the hall, out of the front door, through the grounds up towards the landing pad.

Before she reached it, the helicopter had landed, the blades still rotating, but the men in the machine were clambering out, heads bent, hurrying out of range before they stood upright.

Saskia's eyes flicked eagerly from one to the other of them; mostly they were in uniform, the familiar *carabinieri* uniform, military, all shiny buttons and boots, guns on their hips. There was only one man not in uniform. For a second she almost didn't recognise him. He was muddy and unshaven, his clothes torn and dirty, hair dishevelled, face grimy, a bruise on his forehead, another on his cheek, the flesh along the cheekbone glazed, swollen, with the dark angry red of a cut inside the bruise.

She took all that in as she ran towards him, sobbing.

Domenico caught her in his arms and held her, so tightly she could scarcely breathe, but that didn't matter, nothing mattered, except that he was alive, and safe.

CHAPTER NINE

'I DIDN'T actually see Claudia while they were keeping me in an old shepherd's hut up in the mountains,' Domenico explained later in the salon. The police had all left; they would be coming back, to take further statements from Domenico, but for the moment they were leaving the Alessandros family a little time alone, and Anna and Guido wanted to hear the whole story of what had happened from Domenico himself.

'Then how did you guess she was involved?' Saskia asked, bewildered.

He grimaced. 'I recognised her husband's voice. He stayed away from me as much as possible, but I overheard him talking outside the hut. Salvatore Agnelli masterminded the whole operation. He's a very dominating personality; not good-looking, but he has these fixed eyes, hypnotic, a bit crazy but women find him sexy, maybe because he scares them and they like that?'

Saskia shivered. 'Not me! I don't enjoy being scared; I don't know anyone who does.'

'Well, Agnelli had his two younger brothers under his thumb, and Claudia too, from the minute she met him—and her cousin, Carlo, who was once in the air force, and could fly helicopters. That was essential; you can see why. They had to have someone to pilot the helicopter; their whole scheme depended on that. They knew they didn't have a chance of getting past my bodyguards in the normal way; they needed the element of surprise. I wouldn't be expecting my own pilot to attack me, and neither would my men. Carlo Forli was a brilliant pilot, but he had a drink problem. He was dishonourably dis-

147

charged from the air force for manslaughter. He served ten years in prison for flying when he was blind drunk; he crashed and killed several people. He was lucky they didn't throw away the key. It was only his previous record in the service that saved him. But he was very bitter about the whole thing and ready to throw in his lot with this little gang led by Agnelli.'

'But Claudia went along with it all? She knew what was going on?' Anna asked and her brother nodded at her, his mouth indenting.

'I don't think there's any doubt about it. They got all their information from her. She knew my entire routine. She could break into my computers, she knew my codes, most of all she knew Luca, my pilot. She visited him at some stage, out of the blue, and while he was out of the room she planted a bug in his phone, so that if I rang up to give him orders they always knew about it. They were clever; but then Claudia is clever; I never doubted that. Together she and Agnelli were a dangerous team. They had this planned for months ahead. They didn't make the mistake of rushing it, and in case the police got on to Claudia she was careful to set up her alibi for yesterday.'

Saskia frowned. 'But they can't have known in advance that you would ring your pilot and ask him to take you to Padua!'

Domenico gave her a sideways look. 'Well, yes, they did. You see, I rang my pilot the morning I saw you in the Accademia, and told him to stand by next afternoon to come and pick me up.'

Her blue eyes dark, she said, 'Are you saying you always meant to take me off to see your father? It wasn't just a sudden decision?'

'I knew how much it would mean to him to get a chance to tell you he was sorry,' Domenico quietly said.

'Did you tell your pilot that Saskia was back and would be coming?' asked Anna and her brother shook his head.

'I never mentioned her. Just said I wanted to go to Padua next afternoon. So Claudia went off to a market at Verona, to buy farm-made cheese and bread, and had lunch there, at a crowded restaurant, making sure lots of people saw her, talked to her. Her husband and his brothers were, supposedly, off fishing, up near Lake Garda. They set up an alibi too, in the early morning, arguing on a riverbank, then Agnelli stayed there, to provide cover, while the others slipped away and drove off in an old builder's van, knocked out my pilot and stole my helicopter. They snatched me and flew west across the Po valley to the foothills and abandoned the helicopter, locked me in the boot of another car which was hidden among some trees, and drove me up to the hut.'

'I still don't understand how the police found you so quickly,' Saskia said, sitting curled up next to him on the brocade-covered sofa, her body resting against him.

'Captain Rosi tells me it was good police work,' Domenico said, his lips twitching in amusement. 'He still doesn't believe in telepathy, by the way.'

'What? After we proved...'

'He doesn't admit we proved anything. I told him I believed we could talk to each other in our minds and he laughed and said that if his wife were as beautiful as mine he would agree with her however crazy she was! Just to keep her happy.'

Flushed, Saskia seethed. 'But if I hadn't told him about Claudia...'

'He thinks your female instincts were working there. You were jealous of Claudia so you guessed she was involved somehow, and you just happened to be right!'

'Oh, really!' Saskia ground out between her teeth.

'Well, it seems they had suspected from the start that I was being held in the Dolomites because the helicopter had been abandoned close to the foothills. But it is a big area to search on foot; it was useful to know about

Claudia because it made sense for whoever snatched me to be hiding within an easy driving distance of their own home so that supplies could be brought in without arousing too much suspicion, should the negotiations take a long time. In fact, they had plenty of food and drink for at least a week and Claudia had been ordered not to go near the hut. But it wasn't very far away, all the same. A matter of miles, that's all. Once they pinpointed Salvatore Agnelli's house they brought in police spotter planes which flew in circles radiating outwards from the house, right over that area, using nightsight cameras to take photographs of every isolated building.'

'Wouldn't that have alerted the kidnappers, though?' asked Guido, frowning.

'That was a risk, but then the kidnappers would have expected the police to look for me in the mountains, and by flying at night it made it harder for the men in the hut to be sure what was going on. They were trusting to the fact that the Dolomites cover such a wide area that it could take weeks to search it properly.'

'So how did they actually pin-point the hut?' asked Anna.

'The police had foot patrols of local policemen going around asking questions about Claudia and her husband; what they did, where they went, if anyone had seen them driving in the mountains and if so in what direction. There is always gossip in these isolated places; people see far more than you would expect and they talk about what they notice. Someone had seen Agnelli on a remote mountain road; the police went over the aerial photographs again, noticed an abandoned shepherd's hut up there, and saw it was showing light at night, which meant someone was using it. They arrived just before dawn, mob-handed. They were armed—just as well, because the kidnappers resisted. I was asleep when shooting broke out. I knew it had to be the police. I was in a tiny room with shutters over the windows, held in place by iron bars on the other side. I couldn't see anything much, I couldn't get out, I could only wait. I was deeply relieved when it was the police who came through the door. Quite literally came through it, by the way—half a dozen of them crashed it and the whole door fell into the room with the police on top of it.'

'But none of the kidnappers was killed?' Guido asked.

'Wounded, but not killed; they'll live to stand trial.'

'And they picked up Claudia and her husband?'

'Yes, I saw them briefly, at the police station when I was making my statement.' His face tightened, dark red. 'Claudia screamed abuse at me; I'd no idea she hated me that much.'

There was a brief silence, then, 'Hell hath no fury like a woman scorned,' Saskia said in English.

Domenico grimaced. 'I'm afraid you could be right.'

Anna and Guido exchanged a look. 'Well, thank God you came out of it OK,' Anna said, getting up. 'At least we didn't have to pay that massive ransom to get you back!' She laughed and her brother gave her a wry look.

'They wouldn't have released me if you had paid, you know. They'd have killed me.'

Saskia shivered.

'I'm glad they didn't,' Anna said, kissing her brother.

'We're going home to our children, but if you need us just give us a ring,' Guido said. 'You two need some peace and quiet, I think, don't you?'

Domenico grinned at him. 'I think you're right.'

'You won't forget to visit Papà, will you?' Anna reminded him as they walked to the door, where she hugged them both. 'I'm glad to have you both back,' she whispered to Saskia. 'I missed you; don't go away again, will you?'

Saskia wanted to cry. Instead she said huskily, 'Thank you for being such a tower of strength throughout all this! I don't know what I'd have done without you.'

'Oh, you'd have coped,' said Anna firmly. 'You look fragile, but you're stronger than you look.'

When Anna and Guido had gone, Saskia huskily said, 'I must ring Jamie, let him know what's been happening; he must think...'

'That you have decided to stay with me,' Domenico said softly.

'But I haven't!' She was in a state of such confusion and uncertainty that her voice shook, but she faced him, chin up. 'Domenico, don't try to push me into any snap decisions! The last twenty-four hours have been a terrible trauma for both of us. It would be stupid of me to make any rash promises to you just because of what's happened. The underlying problems between us haven't gone away. I don't belong here. We're such different people, from such different worlds.'

'Yet you read my mind and despite what Captain Rosi thinks you may have saved my life,' he reminded, his eyes insistent. 'Even when we're miles apart the link between us still holds. I think it always will, Saskia. Body and soul, we belong together, whatever you say. You can't leave me again; I won't let you.'

He was so pale and haggard, even though he had changed his clothes, shaved, showered, and looked far more normal than he had when he first got back. The last twenty-four hours had been a traumatic ordeal; he must have been afraid he was going to be killed at any moment. Pity moved inside her like pain.

'You ought to go to bed, Domenico, have a long rest,' she said.

'And have you vanish while my back is turned? Oh, no, Saskia.' He looked at his watch. 'I suggest we go and visit my father.'

'The police told you to stay put!'

'I don't take orders from policemen.'

'But, Domenico...'

'Don't argue with me, Saskia! I want you to see my father, listen to what he has to say. It may make you see things differently.'

She didn't want to go, but how could she refuse to do what he wanted? She kept looking at him and thinking, He's alive. Thank God, he's alive, and safe.

They went by car, not helicopter; Adriano drove them and they had the usual escort of bodyguards in another car.

'Tomorrow I must visit Leo and Enrico in hospital,' Domenico said as they drove through the flat green valley fields towards Padua. 'The police say they'll both pull through, but they are going to be in hospital for a long time, I'm afraid.'

Saskia wasn't listening; she was staring out of the window at the landscape dreaming in golden light around them, the valley criss-crossed with rivers and streams, set in rushes and water meadows. She was too busy to notice anything she saw; she was fighting a panic fear which made her skin cold, her hair prickle on the back of her neck.

What was Giovanni going to say to her? How would he look at her? Should she have told Domenico what happened on that last day in their Milan home?

She had been alone in the house, apart from Giovanni Alessandros, who was in his own room, and the servants, who were out of earshot in the kitchen quarters.

Saskia had been lying down on her bed; the family doctor was keeping her tranquillised but the last dose had worn off and she had been restlessly agitated. She had begun to wander around the house like a lost soul, and had finally opened the door of the lemon-walled nursery which had only a fortnight earlier been decorated ready for the birth of her child.

Giovanni had ordered that. Saskia had superstitiously felt it was far too early to make preparations, but the old man had overruled her, and now grief swept through her with unbearable intensity.

The room had mocked her—all the pretty white furniture with its cheerful stencils of nursery-rhyme characters, the hanging mobile of birds over the cot, the toys on shelves, the nursery lamps, to give a diffused and gentle light at night, the bright curtains and soft-piled carpets.

It would have been the room in the house she loved most, been happiest in, if her child had been born alive; now she couldn't bear to see it.

She had begun to dismantle the cot in frantic, trembling haste. She had stacked it in a corner for someone to take away, then begun to empty piles of new baby clothes from a chest of drawers. Everything could go to a charity or children's hospital, she'd thought, her hands trembling, and it was while she was doing that that Giovanni had come into the room.

'What are you doing?'

His harsh, grating voice had made her jump, but she hadn't looked at him.

'I'm clearing the room. I want everything taken away.' Her own voice sounded odd, even to her; staccato, strained.

'Leave his things alone! Don't you touch my grandson's things; get your hands off them! You killed him! You couldn't even give us a child; God knows why Domenico married you.'

Stricken, she had looked round at him then. As her dilated blue eyes stared back at him the old man's face had contorted into a mask of hatred.

'My son should never have married you! I told him he was making the biggest mistake of his life, but he wouldn't listen! I said to him, Who is she? Who are her people? What do we know about her? She has no money, no family, nothing! But no, Domenico wouldn't listen—— ''She will give me sons'', he said. And what have you given him? Nothing but grief.'

It was true. What could she say?

So she didn't answer at all. She just stood there, helpless, dumb, pitying the old man, filled with a grief that matched his, suffering.

Her silence seemed to infuriate him; but then everything she had ever said or done had made him angry.

She could never have said the right thing, done the right thing, with Giovanni. He had hated her the minute he set eyes on her. He was a proud man, obsessed with his family, with the past, arrogant, scornful. He had never understood why his son had married someone like her. Even when Domenico said he loved her it only made his father angrier; Giovanni had resented that love, been jealous of her.

He got hold of her neck and began to shake her violently, shouting at her. 'I'd like to kill you! I'd like to kill you!'

She didn't struggle or try to get away; a sort of fatalism paralysed her.

Suddenly Giovanni's hands slackened; he looked down at her with glaring, half-blind eyes, muttered something in Italian, which she didn't catch, then threw her away from him and, breathing heavily, lurched out of the room.

Only when he had gone did Saskia come out of her strange trance; only then did she start to realise what had almost happened—that she had, in effect, consented to her own death, become the old man's accomplice to her own murder.

That was when she began to be afraid; and with fear came revulsion, and the realisation that she must get away, that she couldn't stay here.

It wasn't so much that she was afraid of her father-in-law, although she had always been scared of him, even more now, with good reason—but she was far more afraid of what might happen next time, not only for herself, but for everyone else, including Giovanni.

If he had actually killed her just now the consequences for himself, for Domenico, for the whole Alessandros family, would have been catastrophic.

The best he could have hoped for was a life sentence in prison, which would have meant, in effect, that he would die there. Perhaps even worse was the scandal and shame he would have had to bear.

Saskia had already brought terrible grief to Domenico; she could not bear to add shame to what he had already suffered. She knew at that moment that she must go away, at once, and never come back.

It had not been easy to get away. Their wealth made them a target, they had to protect themselves. The house was a fortress, as hard to get out of as it was to get into, bristling with security devices and hidden cameras, and guarded day and night by security men.

Saskia had had to invent a lie. She had said she wanted to go shopping, had been escorted as usual by a couple of bodyguards. First she had visited her bank and withdrawn a large sum of money. Domenico had always been very generous to her; the bank had shown no glimmer of suspicion. She had then managed to give the bodyguards the slip in a department store in Milan and had fled, in what she stood up in, since she had not dared pack a case. All she had done was slip into her handbag her British passport, and her cheque-book and credit cards.

She had taken a taxi to the airport, was lucky enough to get a seat on a plane leaving almost at once, using cash to pay for the ticket. She had been on edge until the instant that the plane took off.

At Heathrow she had had some more bad moments, afraid that by now Domenico would know she had gone and would have contacted detectives in London, who might be at the airport to meet her plane, but once she was in a taxi and speeding away from the airport into anonymity she had felt much safer and had begun to think out her plans for the future.

She had looked for a job in a part of England she didn't know, and found one easily enough. Luckily, Jamie hadn't asked for references; he had been pleased to find someone who was enthusiastic about gardening and knew what she was doing.

'We're just a couple of miles from Padua now,' Domenico said beside her, making her jump.

She looked blankly at him. 'Oh... are we?'

'We're going straight to see my father. The nursing home is only a short drive from here.'

'He does know we're coming?'

Her nervous voice betrayed her. Domenico gave her a sharp, searching look.

'Of course. I spoke to him on the car phone ten minutes ago, weren't you listening?'

She shook her head, then nodded as she vaguely remembered the phone call. 'Sorry, I was thinking about something else.'

Domenico watched her, said very quietly, 'Why don't you tell me, Saskia?'

'Tell you what?' Nervously, she looked away out of the window; they were driving very fast along a wide road. In the distance she saw the huddled red roofs and pale houses of Padua itself and dominating the skyline a beautiful mirage-like cluster of domes and towers, like minarets, piercing the blue afternoon.

'What's that?' she breathed and Domenico glanced at it.

'The Santo. It's the biggest church in Padua; it was built in the early thirteenth century, to hold the relics of St Anthony.'

'It looks sort of... Turkish...' The building reminded her of a mosque.

'Byzantine,' agreed Domenico. 'Possibly influenced by the architecture of San Marco, in Venice.'

'That's older?'

'By several centuries. San Marco was first built in the ninth century, a smaller church then; it burnt down, and was replaced, and that was pulled down in the eleventh century, because Venice was becoming far more important, and wanted a bigger church; that's when the present building went up; and the architect was Greek, which is why it has that oriental look to it. Since then, of course, all sorts of additions have been made to it— San Marco of today is a patchwork of bits from every century, but that's half its charm.'

She gave him a thoughtful look, a faint smile curling her mouth. 'You love living so close to Venice, don't you?'

He grinned at her. 'Yes, I love the place, although I think I'm glad I don't live in the city. Most of the year it's overrun with tourists and when the mist closes in the airport is sometimes closed. I prefer to live on the mainland, but close enough to be able to visit Venice by boat whenever I feel like it. If the weather is good I fly from Venice Airport; if there are any problems I can go by helicopter to another airport and fly from there, or else go by car.'

Talking about Venice was helping to keep her mind from where they were going, so that she didn't have to think about Giovanni Alessandros, and distracting Domenico from his questions about his father, too.

A few minutes later, the limousine slowed and turned in at massive stone gates. Saskia looked up at the white façade of the large nineteenth-century house which had become a private nursing home. It was framed in shrubberies: dark green laurels, bay trees, juniper and cypress. As the car drew up in front of the house a woman in white, wearing a stiffly starched uniform and cap, came out and waited for them to descend, her oval face surveying them calmly, any curiosity she felt hidden from sight.

'He's waiting very impatiently for you,' she said in Italian to Domenico. 'Please don't stay too long; he is far too excited. You know we have to be careful; too much excitement is bad for his heart.'

'I'll be careful, Sister,' Domenico promised. 'This is my wife, by the way. Saskia, this is Sister Rovigo.'

Shyly, Saskia tried a little smile on the other woman, who gave her a nod, shook hands with her briskly, showing no sign of knowing anything about her, although she obviously knew that Saskia and Domenico had been separated for a long time. If she wondered what Saskia was doing here, or whether she and Domenico were back together again, she hid her curiosity well. No doubt the ability to be smoothly discreet was part of her required skills for this job.

'I'll come along to his room with you just to check on him, then I'll come back in ten minutes,' was all she said.

They followed her into the house and across a hall whose floor was paved in black and white diamond marble tiles, along a wide corridor which ended in a glass door through which could be seen a conservatory full of green ferns and hothouse plants.

The sister paused at a door, knocked on it.

'Come in!'

Saskia drew a shaken breath as she recognised the deep, harsh tones. She could never forget the voice of Giovanni Alessandros. She had hoped she would never hear it again.

Fear made her almost sick.

The ward sister opened the door and walked into the room saying cheerfully, 'Here they are, Signor Alessandros! You can stop fretting now. I told you they'd be here any minute, didn't I? But I've told them they can only stay a short time; you mustn't tire yourself.'

Saskia couldn't move.

Domenico was watching her. She knew his attention was focused on both her face and her mind; he could read both, and she had no hiding place from him. She was beginning to see why her friends at school had been so upset when she told them what they were thinking. It was unnerving, disturbing, especially when you were in emotional turmoil and trying to stabilise yourself.

'Don't worry, I'll be with you,' he said, his voice low enough for the others inside the room not to hear him. His hand caught hers, held it firmly, refused to let go when she tried to pull away.

He urged her forward and she let him lead her towards the bed, the narrow, white-covered bed, in which the old man lay.

One glance and Saskia felt a stab of shock as she saw the change in him since they last met. Her fear fell away—she stopped thinking about herself; she was too overcome with pity for Giovanni.

He was very close to death. There was no question now about what Domenico had told her. She could see it was true. It was written in his face, the blueness around his mouth, the gauntness of worn flesh, fallen in on its bones, the lines of pain bitten into the skin.

The deep-sunk, lightless dark eyes were fixed on her. She had never imagined she would see that expression in them. No pride, no arrogance now. Pleading.

His mouth moved but no sound came out. He held out a hand that trembled visibly, and without even thinking Saskia pulled free of Domenico, walked over to the bed and took the withered hand in both her own.

The ward sister had left the room, closing the door quietly behind her. Domenico stood at the foot of the bed, watching his father and Saskia.

'How are you?' she gently asked Giovanni.

His lips moved again; this time she heard one word. 'Forgive...'

She didn't hesitate. 'Yes,' she whispered, and pressed his hand.

As if exhausted, he closed his eyes, sighing.

Domenico brought over a chair, touched her shoulder to tell her it was there. She sat down, still holding his father's hand because the worn fingers gripped hers tenaciously. Domenico moved another chair closer so that he could see both their faces. She was very conscious of his attention, although she didn't look at him.

'Domenico took so long choosing a wife,' Giovanni murmured so quietly she had to bend closer to hear him. 'I was angry with him. There were plenty of suitable women... beautiful girls from good families. Why couldn't he marry one of them? The years were flashing by, and I was afraid I'd die before I saw a grandson from him. Oh, my daughters had children, but I wanted a grandson from my son; I wanted our name to go on. Our family name is two thousand years old. It must not die out. And then he brought you home.'

He lay still, breathing stertorously, and her anxiety deepened. He looked so ill, as if he might die at any minute.

She looked sideways at Domenico, her blue eyes wide, apprehensive.

He bent and picked up his father's wrist, felt for his pulse, and Giovanni's lids lifted; he looked at his son, his smile wry, weary.

'I was just resting. Talking tires me.'

'Then don't talk, Papà.' Domenico was frowning.

'I must,' the old man said, shifting restlessly in the bed. 'It is probably my last chance. I don't want to die with her on my conscience.'

Saskia pressed the worn fingers she still held and he looked from his son's face to her again. She quietly smiled at him.

'You needn't have me on your conscience. I'm not in
any difficulties. You can stop blaming yourself...for...for anything.'

'I drove you away.'

'No,' she lied, then realised that it was not, in fact, a
lie. 'I would have gone, anyway,' she added, and that
was the truth. Giovanni had precipitated things, but she
would have gone, even if he had not attacked her. Her
marriage to Domenico had reached a crisis point. She
couldn't have borne to go on living with him once she
had lost her baby.

The stress of her situation had been too much. She
had been living with a sense of inferiority, of alienation,
isolation for too long; she had had to go or die.

Giovanni sighed. 'You are being kind to me. I don't
deserve it, especially after what I did to you that day
you left. I know I frightened you. I frightened myself.
I hadn't meant to...I was horrified by what I'd done.
I've never struck a woman before in my life; I couldn't
believe I'd done that.'

'Forget about it, please, just forget about it!' Saskia
felt Domenico's tense attention beside her, the stiffening
of his body just now when he heard what Giovanni had
said, those hard grey eyes flicking from her face to his
father's.

'How can I forget I attacked you?'

'You weren't yourself; you were in shock,
after...after...' Tears stung her eyes.

Giovanni made a low, harsh sound, tightening his grip
on her hand. 'So were you. What I said was cruel and
untrue, and I knew it even while I was saying it. You
had just been through a terrible experience; you were as
much in shock as I was...I've no excuse for what I did.
I went crazy for a little while; I blamed you for everything, I wanted to kill you, and then when I found out
you had run away I felt terrible; I knew you had gone
because of what I'd done to you. I would have come

looking for you myself, but I had a heart attack the same day.'

She nodded. 'Domenico told me. I'm very sorry.'

Giovanni looked from her to his son. 'You kept asking me what I had said to her to make her leave, but I couldn't bear to tell you. Now you know.' His face quivered. 'I told her it was her fault she lost her baby. I've been haunted by her face ever since. She was so white, so stricken. I looked at it and somehow her pain just made me angrier. I wanted to hurt her. I can't remember exactly what I did...hit her, shook her...' He groaned. 'God knows. I was out of my mind; I ended up almost choking her, and then I suddenly realised what I was doing. I walked out without telling her I was sorry, although I was, even then. That's why she ran away, Domenico. I drove her away.'

Domenico's face was rigid, mask-like; it was impossible to tell what he was thinking from that face but Saskia picked up the fierce leap of emotions inside him. Domenico had guessed that his father had said unkind things to her, but he hadn't suspected that Giovanni had physically attacked her; shock was reverberating inside him.

She knew how he felt because it echoed her own resentment and shock whenever she thought about her father-in-law and what he had said and done to her that day, all the days before that. He had been her enemy from the moment they met.

All that seemed so far away now. It was over; the hatred had gone from his face, the bitterness from his eyes. He was a different man; burnt-out, all emotion spent, hanging on to life by a mere thread.

'So that was why she was afraid of coming to see you,' Domenico said in a low, flat voice.

His father nodded. Didn't speak. He was watching his son, too, his eyes afraid. Giovanni loved his only son with a feeling that was deeper than logic; Domenico was the future, was to carry on the family name, the family blood. That was vital to a man like Giovanni Alessandros, who had grown up believing that family was all-important. He had been fond of his daughters but they had never seriously mattered; they were females and he needed a male heir. He had put everything of himself into the son who appeared at last, after years of disappointment; all his love had gone to his only son. Now he had to face the possibility of losing Domenico's love because of what he had done to Saskia, and Giovanni was more afraid of that than of death itself.

Saskia's bitterness towards Giovanni had died at the moment when she saw death written in his face.

She had never really hated the old man, anyway. Hate was not in her nature, did not come easily to her. She had simply reacted to his hatred. Now she knew that he no longer hated her, that he was sorry for what he had done to her, she felt her anger and fear vanish.

'I said I forgave him; I meant it,' she told Domenico.

'Can you forget it too?' His face and voice were grim.

She didn't give him a direct answer. 'Don't put all the blame on your father! What he said and did that last day wasn't the only reason why I went!'

'But what he did was the last straw!' Domenico bitterly said, and he was right, of course.

'It was the trigger,' she said, then looked at Giovanni, who was listening, his face white, his lips blue, his eyes dark. 'That's all it was, the trigger. I would have gone, anyway, without that, but I might not have gone just then.'

'We all treated you badly,' Giovanni said wearily. 'And that was my fault. My daughters took their cue from me; they always do. If I'd made you welcome, they'd have done the same.'

The door opened and the ward sister bustled forward, her white skirts rustling.

'I'm sorry, but I'm afraid I must ask you to leave now, Signor Alessandros,' she said to Domenico, her eyes on his father, frowning at the pallor, the strained breathing of the old man. 'Your father must rest. Visits tire him.'

Giovanni clutched Saskia's hand. 'Will you come again?' he whispered. 'There is a lot I still want to say to you.'

She hesitated, knowing she would be going back to England next day, then met his pleading eyes, saw the foreknowledge of death inside them, and was filled with compassion. How could she refuse?

Domenico didn't wait for her to make up her mind. Calmly he said, 'We'll come again tomorrow, Papà.'

Saskia didn't argue, not in front of his father. She would talk to Domenico when they were alone. Bending, she kissed Giovanni softly on the cheek, murmured something vague about seeing him soon, and followed Domenico out of the room.

'I can't come again,' she muttered as she walked out of the nursing home with him. 'I'm going back to England.'

'You promised him you would.' His grey eyes challenged her, cool and insistent.

She was distraught. 'I couldn't say no when he looked at me like that, but... I can't stay on here...'

'You promised him you'd come tomorrow,' Domenico stubbornly repeated.

The limousine was waiting for them; Domenico put her into it and joined her. As the car pulled away they were both silent, aware of the chauffeur only a few feet away.

Saskia stared out of the window, suddenly realising that while they were in the nursing home the weather had abruptly changed. The sky had darkened, was heavy with rain clouds.

A few moments later, they drove into a belt of heavy rain. Great puddles had already formed on the roads, trees lashed backwards and forwards in the wind, visibility was low; the car slowed to a crawl as traffic choked the road in front of it.

A roll of thunder made her jump and peer out anxiously at the sky. The lightning flash followed so soon on the heels of the thunder that it was clear the storm was near by.

Nervously, she said, 'Is it safe to drive in a thunderstorm as bad as this?'

Domenico looked out of the window, frowning at the dark clouds. 'It would be safer not to!' he admitted, grimacing. 'But this storm should soon blow over. Weather changes fast at this time of year. These spring storms can be violent, but they're usually quite short.'

Saskia hoped he was right; she was frightened of thunderstorms and did not want to drive through one.

Domenico glanced at her, then smiled, catching her hand and holding it tightly, his fingers cool and firm.

'I'd forgotten you were afraid of storms! Don't worry. I've never heard of a car being hit by lightning!'

Saskia didn't look convinced.

As they inched slowly along the road behind a string of other vehicles the storm grew louder, more violent.

'We're driving right into it!' she whispered, jumping at the crash of thunder, which had the staccato sound of the automatic weapons the kidnappers had used.

Domenico frowned, and she knew he had picked up what she was thinking about.

'You're safe with me, darling; don't even think about all that.'

How could she help it?

The flash of the lightning split the sky in two and lit up the darkened landscape for a few seconds every time; the rain cascaded endlessly, gutters overflowed, fields running from each side of the road were turning into shallow lakes, the windscreen-wipers on the limousine couldn't cope with the water running down the glass which made the chauffeur slow even more, peering uneasily ahead.

Domenico suddenly leaned forward, tapped on the glass and spoke to him in terse Italian. There was a roll of thunder at that minute; Saskia didn't catch what Domenico had said.

As he sat back beside her the car took a right-hand turn, off the main road, into what looked like a driveway. Startled, Saskia turned to Domenico, her blue eyes alarmed.

'Where are we going?'

'This is a hotel; I've sometimes had lunch here when I was visiting my father.'

'A hotel?' She sat up, her face stiffening. 'I'm not going to a hotel with you.'

'You prefer to drive through the storm?'

She looked back at the totally blocked lines of traffic they had left behind, which had now stopped moving altogether, and bit her lip.

Softly, Domenico said, 'I suggest we have lunch, then drive back when the storm is over.'

She could see the hotel building now, a small eighteenth-century villa set in trees. The lights shining from it were very welcoming, inviting, as they cut through the darkness of the storm.

'At least we'll be warm and dry in there,' Domenico pointed out. 'It's small, but they have a charming salon for the guests to sit in, a bar, and a pretty dining-room. The owners run it themselves. He inherited it; it's a family home. You may not meet him, but he does all the cooking, and he's good, believe me. I've eaten very well here. It isn't cordon bleu, the food is provincial Italian, and first-rate. His wife runs the place. They're usually full, and it's very late for lunch, but they know me; I'm sure they'll find us something to eat.'

'But it will be very late before we get to Venice!' she protested. 'I know I have to stay on here to be available for police questioning, but I wanted to see Jamie before he leaves.'

Domenico's black brows met in a jagged line. 'Damn Jamie.'

The fierce snarl made her nerves jump, but she snapped back at him.

'I should never have come with you!'

His face darkened. 'It isn't my fault that we ran into a storm.'

'Maybe it isn't,' she said, scowling at him. 'But you aren't exactly sorry, either, are you?'

'What do you want me to do—pretend I'm not looking forward to having lunch alone with you?'

His grey eyes stared down into hers and she looked away, very flushed. Her heart was racing, she felt oddly dizzy. To calm herself down she stared out of the car window.

The grounds of the hotel seemed extensive; a tennis court, the wire netting around it rattling, an empty swimming-pool whose surface was dimpled by rain, beautifully kept lawns and flowerbeds, cypresses swaying violently to and fro in the wind. There wasn't a soul in sight; any guests must be safely indoors.

They drew up outside the front entrance, which was under a portico; the chauffeur came round and opened the door. Domenico got out and helped Saskia to descend, hurried her into the house so that she didn't get wet, merely felt the driving wind tug at her hair, her clothes, stinging her cheeks like a flail.

A woman in her late twenties with glowing apricot skin and smooth dark hair sat behind a desk in the tiled reception hall. She looked up as she heard their arrival, her face surprised, then smiled, black eyes lighting up at the sight of Domenico, and came quickly over to shake hands with him.

'We haven't seen you for some time! How are you? Has this terrible weather driven you in here for shelter from the storm? I don't blame you! I've just been thinking how glad I am that I don't have to go out in it.'

Even while she talked in her honey-warm Italian voice, her black eyes were flicking to Saskia from time to time, obviously curious. Had Domenico ever brought a woman here before?

That idea made Saskia's whole body wince in pain, with a stab of fierce jealousy. Had Domenico had other women during the last two years? She hadn't asked him. She was afraid of the answer, but it had been on her mind all these months; it was there now.

He looked round at her at that moment, his grey eyes narrowed, glittering, piercing her face. She looked down, very pale, her hands clenched at her sides.

Whatever he had picked up from her, he went on talking to the hotel receptionist in a calm tone.

'It's like Noah's flood out there; it doesn't look as if it is ever going to stop raining. We're driving back to Venice, but it was impossible to drive through this storm!'

Every note of his voice made her senses beat like candle-flames in the wind. Love consumed her. The very idea of leaving him again was unendurable—yet the idea of staying was just as bitter. She was in torture.

Quietly, he said, 'Oh, you haven't met my wife, have you, Caterina? Saskia, this is Caterina Manzini. She and her husband own the hotel. Anna, this is my wife, Saskia.'

If Caterina Manzini knew that Domenico and his wife had been separated for a long time she gave no hint of curiosity, merely shook hands and smiled warmly at Saskia.

'So, we meet you at last. We know your husband well, of course; he often comes when he is visiting his father. You have been to visit old Signor Alessandros? How is he?'

'Very frail,' Saskia said on a sigh.

'He has lived longer than we dared hope for after he had his first attack,' Domenico said.

A loud roll of thunder made them all look round towards the door as it opened, and the chauffeur hurried into the hall, followed by the two bodyguards.

They shook themselves on the mat like dogs on a wet day, bowed to Caterina Manzini and walked off purposefully. Obviously Domenico had often stopped off here on his way to and from the nursing home, and the men knew their way around the hotel.

'They'll get some pasta in the kitchen,' Caterina Manzini told Saskia, seeing her stare after the men. 'They usually do while your husband is eating in the restaurant.' Then she frowned, looking at the large book open on the desk. 'You were wanting lunch? I am very sorry, we have a problem with that...all the tables are booked for a private party, a local couple celebrating a birthday; they've brought some of their relatives here, most of our rooms are let to them, so the dining-room is shut to everyone else.'

'You couldn't fit us in before their party starts?'

Caterina sighed. 'They will be here shortly, I'm afraid. Look, the best we can do is to send you up lunch in the suite. It's empty, but all the other rooms are taken. We won't charge you for the room, just for the meal.'

She looked from one to the other of them, lifting her dark brows enquiringly.

'Thank you, that's fine,' said Domenico. 'Tell your husband something simple—prosciutto and melon to start with, and then a little grilled breast of chicken with salad? My wife likes chicken.'

Caterina beamed. 'Certainly, I'll ring through to Paolo at once.' She turned and selected a key from the rows behind her. 'Here's the key to the suite. Make yourselves at home. Can I send up anything to drink?'

'White wine, any vintage you know I like, a bottle of mineral water as well, and coffee afterwards.' He glanced at Saskia. 'Shall we have a drink in the bar before dinner? An aperitif?'

She hesitated, more because she didn't want to be alone with him in this suite than because she wanted an aperitif.

'No, maybe not,' Domenico said before she had made up her mind how to answer. 'Thank you, Caterina, we're very grateful; you've saved our lives. By the way, if the weather doesn't improve, we would like to keep the suite for the night; is that possible?'

'Of course!' she smiled.

Saskia was trembling as she walked towards the small lift which she saw facing the hotel desk.

When she and Domenico were shut in it and moving up to the first floor she turned on him fiercely.

'I am not spending the night here with you!'

'What are you going to do, sit outside in the car all night?'

'If I have to!'

'Don't be ridiculous!'

The lift stopped and he waved her out into a wide, elegant corridor. He glanced at the key, checked the number of the room opposite and walked to the left, with Saskia reluctantly following him.

The suite was at the far end; there were double doors which opened into a beautifully furnished apartment with a sitting-room, bathroom and bedroom, all spacious and decorated in a gracious eighteenth-century Italian style, with a lot of gilt and silk brocade.

They both stood in the sitting-room looking around. Outside the rain and wind howled, unabated. They listened to the sound of the storm for a minute; Saskia shivered, and Domenico glanced at her, his mouth mocking.

'Admit it: you would rather be in here than out there!' he drawled.

Obstinately, she said, 'I am not spending the night here with you! Our marriage is over.'

His face tightened, hardened. 'You are not going back to England. You are staying here with me, Saskia!'

Her face white, she confronted him, shaking her head. She had made up her mind; she could not bear to be hurt like that again; their marriage had been a crazy risk and if she had known what lay ahead for her she would never have agreed to marry him at all. She had been young and naïve and blind to everything marriage with a man like Domenico Alessandros would mean, but now that she was aware of the problems she wasn't taking that risk again.

The burnt child feared the fire.

'No!' she said hoarsely. 'Our marriage is over, Domenico. I'm never coming back to you.'

CHAPTER TEN

'OH, YES, you will,' Domenico said very softly. 'Do you really think I'd ever let you go after the way we made love yesterday afternoon?'

Was it only yesterday? So much had happened since. It seemed already a lifetime ago that that heat and desire had overtaken them. She felt a tremor shake her, like an earthquake shaking a city, his sensual memories merging with her own, just as their bodies had merged.

She shut her eyes, pushing the memories and feelings away.

'That doesn't make any difference!' She couldn't let it make a difference. She mustn't let emotion dictate what she did, not this time. She had been too young when they met to have a clue what she was doing. Domenico hadn't explained what she would be taking on if she married him. Perhaps he hadn't quite realised what it would be like for her? After all, he was used to the way he lived—the power of money and position, the society he moved in every day. How could he have understood what an enormous leap it would be for a working girl to find herself in his world? Had the Prince explained to Cinderella what she would be up against if she married him? And how had Cinderella felt after the wedding, anyway? Had she lived happily ever after or had she gone through what Saskia had endured?

'It makes a difference to me,' Domenico drily said. 'Two years is a long time, Saskia. I was afraid you had met someone else. When I saw you with Forster at the opera I thought he must be your lover, and I was sick with jealousy. But once I met him, saw the two of you together, I knew I needn't worry about him. It was obvious he wasn't and never would be your lover. In fact, there has never been anyone else for you, has there, Saskia?'

She refused to answer that, she wasn't betraying herself—but she couldn't meet his eyes, which was betrayal enough to a man as sharp-eyed as Domenico.

'Any more than there has been anyone else for me,' he said huskily, and her heart turned over, but she struggled not to let him get to her.

She had made a sensible decision, a rational, safe decision. She must not allow Domenico to talk her out of it.

He had dominated their relationship from the minute they'd met. He had been older, experienced, sophisticated, self-assured. She had been innocent, naïve, wide-eyed and very young. She couldn't even believe that someone like him could really be serious about someone like her.

They should never even have met. Their worlds were so far apart. It could only have been fate that made sure they would collide quite literally at the Chelsea Flower Show one summer.

Saskia had taken that week in May off from work. She was staying in London at a cheap hotel in Pimlico, which for a girl used to being on her feet all day in the open air, working hard, was a short walk from the Royal Hospital grounds in Chelsea where the scarlet-coated retired soldiers known as the Chelsea Pensioners lived all year round, and where the famous flower show was held annually in May.

She had been one of a little mob of people jostling around for a view of a wonderful display of roses from one of the top growers, when a tall man in front of her had stepped backwards on to her foot.

Saskia had given a cry of pain and staggered. He had turned, looked down at her, his face startled.

'I am sorry, have I hurt you?'

She had noted the foreign accent first, then the amazing good looks: the Mediterranean colouring, black hair, olive skin, the height and powerful build.

She had been stunned by him and had blushed and stammered some incoherent reply while he had stared down at her with fixed attention.

He had insisted on helping her to a nearby bench. 'I think you should take off your shoe so that we can see if I did any harm.'

Saskia had protested she was fine, but he had knelt down and firmly slipped off her shoe, picked up her small foot and examined the toes in their filmy stockings.

'No damage has been done, I think,' he had said, sliding her foot back into her shoe, then he had stood up, smiling.

Saskia had felt her breathing stop.

She had never seen a smile like it. It was like the sun coming up in the middle of the night.

'Let me buy you tea to make up for being so clumsy,' he had said, taking her arm and leading her off to the tea enclosure.

Saskia had been very shy, at first, but he had put her at her ease once they got on to the subject of roses. Her eyes glowing, she had talked about her favourite varieties, and he had listened intently, watching her, his gaze moving from her blue eyes to her mouth, then up to her dark auburn hair. Saskia had been so absorbed in what she was saying that she hadn't picked up any vibes from him; she hadn't had an idea what he was thinking or feeling at that stage.

They had eaten scones and jam, followed by strawberries and cream. Domenico had got cream on the corner of his mouth; Saskia had shyly pointed it out to him and he had leaned forward.

'Would you wipe it off, please?'

Blushing, she had used her napkin to remove it, her eyes fixed on the sexy curve of his lips.

She had been intensely conscious of touching him, of being close to him. Hurriedly, to cover the fact, she had asked where he came from, then said she had never been to Italy, and she had often thought of going there one day, and Domenico had told her she must go, he was sure she would love it.

Saskia had talked about her job in the park; said she loved it, but that her mother had been amazed when she took the job, hadn't believed she could do it.

'What did your father say?'

'He's dead,' Saskia had said flatly.

'I'm sorry,' Domenico had said, still watching her closely. 'Have you any brothers or sisters?'

She had shaken her head.

'What made you take a job as a gardener?' Domenico had asked, and she had shrugged.

'Impulse—jobs aren't easy to find these days, but I saw this one advertised, so I took it. I'm very glad I did. I could probably earn more in an office, but I'd hate it.'

A minute later she had looked at her watch and realised it was almost closing time for the show. She wanted to avoid getting caught in the rush homeward, so she had said she must be going and got up.

'Do you live in London?' Domenico had asked, and she had explained as she was hurrying towards the exit that she was only on holiday there.

'I've always wanted to see the Chelsea Flower Show.'

'You're in London alone?'

Was he shocked? she could remember thinking as she nodded.

'My mother always goes to Eastbourne every year for two weeks; she hates London.'

He hadn't commented. But he had insisted, in spite of her protests, on taking her back to her hotel in a taxi. She had been embarrassed as they drew up outside the shabby terraced building with its yellowed lace curtains and fading paintwork. She had known nothing of Domenico's background yet, but she had already realised that he must have a good income. His manner, his clothes, the way he spoke had all betrayed as much, although as yet Saskia had had no idea how far apart they really were!

'Thank you for the lift,' she had mumbled, diving out of the taxi.

Domenico had called after her, 'How about tomorrow? Are you going to Chelsea again?'

She had shaken her head. 'I thought I'd do some sightseeing.'

'Would you let me come too?' he had asked, and she should have stopped it there and then, refused to meet him again.

She didn't. She had been too taken aback; she had gone carnation-pink and stammered in stupid confusion; and he had said softly, 'I'll pick you up tomorrow morning at ten, in my car.'

That had been the beginning. A chance meeting, followed by a whirlwind romance leaving her with no time to think. She was helplessly in love within days. She knew little more about him than she had in the beginning; she only knew she was crazy about him.

Her holiday had ended, she had gone home, and Domenico had gone back to Italy, but he had rung her every day over the next two weeks, and then he had appeared at her home to meet her mother one weekend. Saskia didn't know who had been more surprised—she, or her mother, who had not been prepared for Saskia to produce such a charismatic man.

Saskia hadn't told her mother much about him, but Mrs Newlyn had been less bemused than her daughter, and far more worldly-wise. She had immediately realised that Domenico was wealthy, and had at first been a little wary, faintly worried about his interest in her daughter.

She had warned Saskia that he might have seduction in his mind; but Saskia was already in love and had just laughed at the idea.

'He isn't like that!'

'All men are!' her mother had said grimly. 'Don't be a silly little goose, Saskia.'

For two days she and Domenico had spent every waking hour together, driving around the country in a hired car, pretending to eat meals neither of them wanted, walking across summer fields, lying together under trees in a woodland glade, listening in rapt silence to the birds and the rustling of the wind in the trees.

Those hours were the happiest she could remember. She had been wildly in love, in a state of hypnotic bliss. Domenico could have slept with her if he had chosen to do so; he could have got her to jump through hoops. She was utterly under his spell.

When he had asked her to marry him she couldn't speak.

'Saskia?' he had asked, framing her face between his hands, looking at her with a fixed intensity that made her heart beat faster. 'Answer me... will you?'

She didn't remember nodding, she certainly hadn't said anything, but the next minute they were kissing, their arms around each other, and she was sure she had died and gone to heaven.

When they broke the news to her mother, she hadn't seemed able to take it in at first, then she had tried to get them to wait, to fix the date for some time in the autumn, or even spring the following year.

Domenico wouldn't hear of it. He wanted to be married immediately.

'What about your own family? They'll want to be there, surely?' her mother had protested.

'I think I ought to meet them,' Saskia had said, nodding.

'My mother is dead, my father never leaves Italy,' Domenico had told them. 'I don't want any fuss. No big wedding. You don't want a big wedding, do you, Saskia?'

Saskia hadn't cared either way, but her mother had been disappointed. Domenico had got his way, though. They had been charmed, coaxed, bulldozed into giving way all along the line. She had married him, only a few weeks later. Her mother had been placated a little by being allowed to choose Saskia a traditional white dress, by the church wedding, by organ music and flowers and some of the trappings her mother had always dreamt she would have, but there had not been any big reception afterwards, just a few friends for lunch at an expensive local hotel, before, promising her mother that she should come and stay with them in Italy later that year, Domenico had taken her off on honeymoon to an enchanting and luxurious villa set among rambling gardens looking down over Lake Como.

Saskia had loved it, but she had also begun to realise slowly that Domenico was keeping a great deal from her. Shyly, she had asked him questions; he had answered economically; bit by bit the truth had begun to dawn on her.

But it wasn't until he took her home to the Alessandros family house at Milan that she realised just how much he hadn't told her.

She had been shattered, and within hours she knew that she had made a terrible mistake. She could not cope with the Alessandros family: with Giovanni's cold pride, with the contempt and arrogance of Domenico's sisters, with the dumb insolence and sneers of the servants who all took their cue from their master, old Giovanni.

The intensity of desire she still shared with Domenico at night in their bedroom couldn't make up for the misery of her days spent in that house while he was away at work for eight or ten hours at a time.

She had run away from him, but she had taken his image with her, in her heart. He was right. There had never been anyone else. There never would be, or could be. She loved Domenico too much; he had ruined her for any other man. They were all tame, dull, predictable compared to him.

She knew why she loved Domenico—but she still couldn't fathom what he saw in her. It had always baffled her; it still did.

He was watching her now, like a hawk on the wing hovering over a mouse in the undergrowth, waiting for a betraying movement, waiting for the right moment to swoop down for the kill.

'Why are you frowning? Don't you believe me? Saskia, there hasn't been anyone else in my life since you left. I've been far too busy hunting for you. Every spare moment I wasn't at work, I spent in England, following up every possibility, however remote.'

There was a tap at the door, a murmured word or two in Italian, and Domenico called, '*Avanti!*'

The door opened. A young woman in a neat black dress came in, wheeling a table covered with a crisp white cloth. The table rattled slightly, loaded as it was with wine glasses, plates, a thin green glass vase holding a single red rose, cutlery, a bottle of wine in an ice bucket, covered dishes.

Domenico spoke to the girl in a friendly way and she answered him, laughed as she set out the table for them, moved chairs up to it.

Saskia slipped off to the bathroom while the table was being made ready. When she returned she found the waitress had opened the wine, poured some into a glass. Domenico tasted it, nodded approval, and she filled two glasses.

Domenico held a chair back for Saskia, who sat down on one side of the table while the waitress was whisking the covers off their food, which was prettily presented on white plates: delicate dark pink slices of cured ham served with thin slices of greeny yellow melon and what looked like peeled pear halves.

'The prosciutto looks good?' the waitress asked and Domenico nodded.

'It looks delicious, and so do the pears.'

'Those are our own pears, preserved in jars by my sister last autumn.'

'Wonderful—please give Caterina my compliments!' Domenico said and the girl smiled.

'I will, thank you. *Buon appetito*! When you are ready for your main course, please ring number seven.'

As the door closed again behind her, Saskia said flatly, 'I ought to ring Jamie, let him know what's happening.'

At once Domenico frowned, and she picked up a jagged flash of jealousy from him, as spiky as the lightning which was still ripping through the sky outside. Impatiently he said, 'It can wait until we've finished our meal! Taste your wine. This is a local wine; you aren't likely to find it anywhere in England, but it is very good. I drink it whenever I'm here; they get it straight from the grower himself; he's a relation of Caterina's. His red wine needs time to mature—I wouldn't drink it for at least four years—but this white is very drinkable when it is only a year or two old.'

She sipped it and nodded. 'Yes, it is good.'

'The pleasure of a good wine is one thing my father really misses,' Domenico said. 'His doctor won't allow him to drink any more.'

Saskia frowned. 'Wouldn't he be happier living with you than in that nursing home?'

'When he got over that first attack he lived with me for a while, and he stayed with my sisters in turn, but he gets weaker all the time, and the trouble is, I have been going away so much, to England, to look for you, or back to Milan, on business. It was decided he needed to be hospitalised so that his condition could be monitored by his specialist, who lives near by. We all visit Papà, and he's comfortable; he seems to like the place.'

Sighing, she asked, 'He knows he's dying, doesn't he?'

Domenico nodded, his face grave. 'That's why he needed to see you; he is clearing all debts before he dies. He doesn't want to leave anything undone. Please don't go back to England, Saskia. Stay, visit my father again. Time is running out for him.'

'I can't,' she wailed. 'Why can't you understand how I feel? I never fitted in with your life. I was a fish out of water, and I always will be. I hate everything about your lifestyle—the stuffy parties, the political talk at dinner-tables, the way your friends all gossip about each other, the way they whisper and giggle over the latest scandal. They don't go to bed until the early hours of the morning, and then they don't get up until lunchtime. They're snobbish and spiteful and shallow, and I never want to see any of them again.'

Domenico's eyes gleamed with amusement and he laughed.

'I wish they could hear you! I'd love to see their faces if they did.'

She shrugged. 'They despise me too much to care.'

'They were jealous of you!'

She stared, dumbfounded, incredulous.

Domenico nodded, face sober. 'Of course they were. If you weren't so wrapped up in your own insecurity you'd know that. You arrived in my life out of the blue, and you were everything they had forgotten how to be— young, gentle, untouched, beautiful. You were a living reproach to them all. You radiated the very spirit of youth—you made their lives seem empty, boring, squalid. I know exactly how they felt because when I first saw you, at the Chelsea Flower Show, I got the same shock. I couldn't believe what I was seeing—the madonna face, the big blue eyes, the sweetness . . . I was so used to a very different sort of woman, and so sick of them all. My family kept suggesting I should marry, but I never liked any of the girls they came up with; none of them was what I was looking for. I didn't ever really know what I did want, only what I didn't... Until I met you and at once I knew you were what I'd been waiting for all those years.'

Saskia bit her lip, staring down at her plate. 'Don't...' she whispered. He was making it so hard for her.

'I'm not going to let you go again, Saskia,' he said flatly.

Tears stung her lids. 'I can't stay...'

She felt his anger, his frustration.

'Eat your prosciutto!' was all he said, though, and she picked up her knife and fork with fingers that trembled.

They ate in silence, not looking at each other, but she knew what he was thinking; she felt the emotions inside him and flinched away from them.

Outside the storm was dying away, although the rain still poured down in sheets; they could hear the gutters overflowing and the windows ran with water.

Domenico rang the waitress who brought their next course and removed their empty plates.

'A tree in the garden was struck by lightning!' she cheerfully said as she served Saskia with her chicken, spooned a mushroom and cream sauce over it. 'We're lucky it was nowhere near the house; it began to burn, but the rain put the fire out before we got there. It will never be the same again, of course; it's half dead, all black and shrivelled.'

Saskia shivered. She had been hit by lightning; she would never be the same again. Her marriage to Domenico had been far too difficult for her to deal with, and losing her baby had crystallised her feelings of inadequacy. She had run away back to England, to be ordinary again, to find some sort of peace and stability in her work, in gardens, in taking care of living, growing things.

The two years since then had given her a chance to heal her wounds, grow as a person, but she still didn't think she was ready to go back to Domenico's world.

Domenico was watching her, his eyes penetrating. As the waitress left again with a loaded tray Domenico put a hand across the table and caught Saskia's shaking fingers between his cool, firm ones.

'Talk to me, darling!'

She started. Their eyes met, the dark images leaping from her to him and back again.

'I couldn't risk having another baby, Domenico!' she whispered.

'I know,' he said gently.

'It hurt too much; I couldn't go through that again; I think I'd go mad if it happened to me again.'

'If you don't feel you're ready to have another child, it doesn't matter,' he soothed.

She couldn't believe him. Wildly, she shook her head.

'You're just saying that now; you don't really mean it.'

Harshly, he said, 'I thought you could see inside my head, Saskia? If you can, you know how much I love you.'

Her face whitened, flamed again, as she felt the emotion beating inside him.

'I've loved you from the minute I saw you,' he said. 'Of course I wanted children, but I want you more. If I have to choose between having children and having you, there's no contest.'

'But your father...'

'I'm not my father! He had an obsession about keeping the family line going. I never did.'

'But you do want children,' she protested, afraid to believe what he was saying.

'I said I did, but if you don't want to risk trying again we won't. My sisters have sons; no doubt one of them would be happy to take the Alessandros name to make sure it goes on. We needn't worry about any of that. All that matters is the two of us, Saskia.'

He lifted her hands to his mouth, kissed her fingers softly.

'Oh, Saskia...I've been very lonely without you. Nothing has mattered since you went. Come back to me, darling.'

She pulled her fingers away and covered her face with both hands. 'I...don't know what to do...don't try to rush me...I can't think straight.'

His voice was quiet, insistent. 'You don't need to think, Saskia. You know how you feel, and if there's one thing I've learnt from all this it's that in the end that's all that really means anything, the way we feel about each other.'

He came round the table, knelt beside her, pulled her hands down and looked deep into her blue eyes.

She was breathing fast, unsteadily. She couldn't get a word out.

He said quietly, 'While you've been away, I've been focusing my mind on you, trying to find you again; I've thought about you so much these past two years, I think I've learnt more about you since you've been gone than I ever did while you were with me. Once I realised what you had been through with my father, my sisters, the servants, I started changing my life, so that when you came back everything would be different. You won't have to put up with any of the problems you had to face before, darling. You needn't see much of my sisters, my father bitterly regrets the way he treated you, and you won't have any trouble dealing with Adriano and his wife. I picked them carefully to make sure of that.'

She wished she could believe him, but she was afraid of making the same mistake twice. 'I'm still not the right sort of wife for a man like you!' she muttered.

His face was stubborn, the hard jaw and mouth tense with determination.

'You're the wife I want.'

'I don't like business people, or dinner parties, or...'

'I don't give a damn about any of that! Saskia, why do you think I never married before? Because I never met a woman I wanted to live with for the rest of my life. I was waiting for someone...I didn't even know who, until I saw you at the Chelsea Flower Show that day in London and it hit me like an arrow out of the dark—you were the woman for me! You still are. My love for you has never changed, Saskia. What was wrong before was that I hadn't really thought about things from your point of view. I was arrogant. I was as much to blame as everyone else for the way you were treated. I married you without realising how hard it was going to be for you to cope with my lifestyle; I just dumped you down into my world and left you to deal with it on your own. When you ran away I had to face up to what I'd been ignoring until then, but I did face up to it, I did deal with it all, Saskia. I promise you, if you come back to me, I'll make sure you never get hurt like that again.'

She sat staring at him, trembling.

Tentatively, she said, 'One of the problems was that I had nothing to do—I didn't have a job, I wasn't allowed to work in the house, I found it hard to make friends. I can't bear to live like that.'

'You will have a job,' he said quickly. 'I want you to work with Pietro, help him bring the gardens back to their original design, re-create a perfect Renaissance garden again.'

She was very still, thinking about it, wondering if he meant this.

Domenico coaxed her some more, knowing that she was listening, taking him seriously, that he had a chance. His voice eager, he promised, 'You won't have anything to do with my business life; there will be no dinner parties, no socialising...I'll work in my office here or go away on business, and you'll work in the gardens; it should take a while to get the place back in shape.'

'Years,' she said, excitement making her eyes bright. 'It's a big job. Are you still planning a rose-garden, or was that just talk?'

Huskily, he said, 'No, I want a rose-garden, and that would be your province, too.' Then he groaned, his face darkly flushed, his eyes glittering, fevered, brilliant. 'Saskia...oh, darling... Darling, make your own terms. Don't you see, that's what I'm saying? I want you back on any terms. You hold all the cards. I can't bear living without you. Stop torturing me. Tell me you'll come back to me.'

Last night there had been a moment when she believed he might be dead.

That shock still reverberated inside her. If he had been dead she knew she wouldn't have wanted to go on living without him.

She loved him. It was crazy to think of leaving him again when every second when they were apart was pure torture.

She couldn't get a word out, she was breathing too fast, her heart beating too hard. But there was no need for words, not between them, not any more. He knew what she was feeling. He knew she would never go away again.

He put his arms around her waist and his head on her lap and knelt there, his body shuddering with relief and passion, and Saskia stroked his hair.

Outside the rain fell and the wind blew; inside the room there was the peace and stillness which followed a hard-fought battle when there was no victor and no vanquished, only lovers who had finally made a truce.

Coming Next Month

HARLEQUIN PRESENTS®

#1767 PRINCE OF DARKNESS Kate Proctor
Damian Sheridan held the key to Ros's past.... But if he discovered her dark secret, would he believe Ros was just an innocent pawn in a game of deceit?

#1768 STRAW ON THE WIND Elizabeth Power
Rex Templeton was rich, gorgeous, charismatic. But he was also paralyzed from the waist down. Could Sasha convince him he was worthy of love?

#1769 THE ALEXAKIS BRIDE Anne McAllister
(Wedlocked!)
Damon Alexakis needed a suitable wife—and Kate needed a pretend lover to keep her matchmaking father happy! The solution? A marriage of convenience for one year only!

#1770 A MASTERFUL MAN Lindsay Armstrong
Davina's handsome new boss, Steve Warwick, was clearly interested in more than Davina's housekeeping skills; could she resist his masterful persuasion?

#1771 CLIMAX OF PASSION Emma Darcy
(Dangerous Liaisons)
When the Sheikh of Xabia accused Amanda of using him to clear her father's name, Amanda proposed a dangerous bargain: one night of love in return for her freedom!

#1772 FANTASIES & AND THE FUTURE Miranda Lee
(Book 4 of Hearts of Fire)
The fourth in a compelling six-part saga—discover the passion, scandal, sin and hope that exist between two fabulously rich families.

Vince Morelli thought Ava was just another rich, lonely housewife looking for fun and thrills! But Ava knew her narrow, virginal existence was gone forever.... Vince was more exciting than any of her fantasies! Life was changing for Gemma, too, but seemingly for the worse: she'd heard evil rumors about Nathan—could they be true?

Take 4 bestselling love stories FREE
Plus get a FREE surprise gift!

Become a Privileged Woman, You'll be entitled to all these Free Benefits. And Free Gifts, too.

To thank you for buying our books, we've designed an exclusive FREE program called *PAGES & PRIVILEGES™*. You can enroll with just one Proof of Purchase, and get the kind of luxuries that, until now, you could only read about.

BIG HOTEL DISCOUNTS

A privileged woman stays in the finest hotels. And so can you—at up to 60% off! Imagine standing in a hotel check-in line and watching as the guest in front of you pays $150 for the same room that's only costing you $60. Your *Pages & Privileges* discounts are good at Sheraton, Marriott, Best Western, Hyatt and thousands of other fine hotels all over the U.S., Canada and Europe.

FREE DISCOUNT TRAVEL SERVICE

A privileged woman is always jetting to romantic places.

When <u>you</u> fly, just make one phone call for the lowest published airfare at time of booking— <u>or double the difference back!</u>

PLUS—you'll get a $25 voucher to use the first time you book a flight AND <u>5% cash back on every ticket you buy thereafter through the travel service!</u>

PROOF OF PURCHASE

Offer expires October 31, 1996

HP-PPS3